By Evan Bond

Smashwords edition
Cover design by Timothy Schmit / Timothyschmit.weebly.com

Evan Bond
Visit my website at www.BookByBond.com

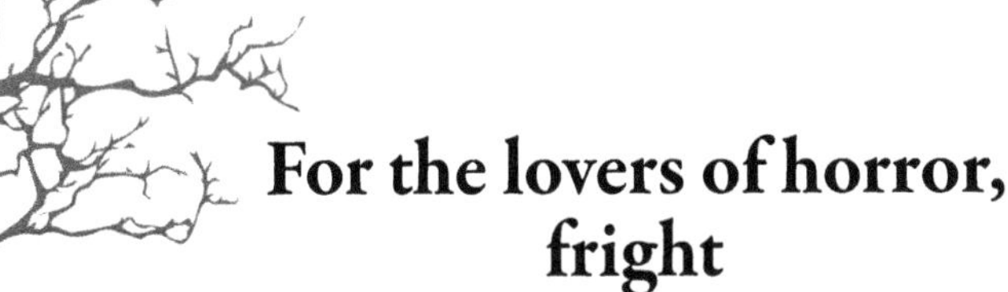

For the lovers of horror,
fright

and all that go bump in the night

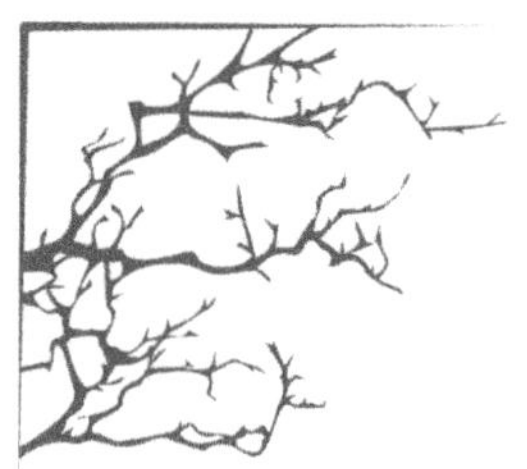

I The Drive

Two vehicles tore down the two-lane highway, forming a small convoy. Far from any town or city, it was unlikely to run across speed traps. Besides the tan Jeep and green SUV, not another car could be seen on the highway. Trees swayed in the breeze on either side of the road with no single man-made structure in sight. It was as far away from civilization most of them had ever been.

Cramped inside the SUV sat four people anxious to get out and stretch their legs. Gas stations were sparse in this country and breaks were too. To make sure they had enough fuel, they kept a red gas canister in the back filled to the brim. It smelled of gasoline in the SUV, but only mildly. Not enough to bother anyone.

“How much longer, Dad?” The young woman in the backseat asked, sounding annoyed. Her parents had insisted she come along on what they called a "family trip." It had only been a few short weeks since she had turned twenty-one and hardly cared for a family vacation. To her, it would have been much more fun to stay at home and get plastered with her friends. When she found out her sister and her husband would be going as well, she decided not to fight it.

“Shouldn’t be too much longer, Ashley.” Her father replied.

“Ashley, if you have to pee you should have done that at the last gas station. Now you’re gonna have to pee in the bushes.” The young man sitting next to her announced.

“Shut up, Wesley,” Ashley yelled back.

“Jeez, you two sound more like teenagers than twenty-somethings.” Their mother said, looking back at them from the passenger seat.

Silence engulfed the car as the siblings stared out the windows in embarrassment. It was several minutes before anyone spoke again. "Can you take a look at the map, Helen? I'm hoping we're almost there."

Helen picked up the map from the dashboard and took a look at it. As she studied it Wesley said, "I can't believe you're using a map. Old school."

"Well," Helen, his mother, responded. "We don't have a GPS signal so we have no other choice. You kids these days don't know how to read a map. You're lucky us old people are still around to show you how. Right, Dan?" Dan laughed as he scanned the road for their turn off. He knew it would be coming soon.

In the following car, a man and woman sat silently as they made their way down the highway. After a few minutes, the man said, "Sweetheart, could you hand me some beef jerky?" She nodded and pulled the bag from the floor. Opening it up, she handed over two pieces of moist jerky. He gobbled it down quickly and thanked her. She helped herself to a few pieces before putting the bag back on the floor.

"Do you think we're almost there, Tyler?"

"Getting bored, Samantha?"

A grin crept across her lips.

"Maybe just a little."

"Well, we're almost there, I think. I mean, we have to be right? We've been driving for like eight hours. We have to be getting close."

As if on cue, the SUV ahead of them began to slow down. The red tail lights burst to life. It was the first man-made light they had seen in hours. "I think this is our turn," Tyler said as he followed Samantha's father onto the dirt driveway.

The ride was bumpy and it took another twenty minutes to finally reach their destination. Samantha looked at it with wonder. It seemed rustic and yet somehow modern. It looked nothing like the cabins she had seen in movies or television shows. Instead, it looked like an average home. Windows in the front, a white garage door on the right side of the home. The concrete walls were painted a hideous yellow and the door was bright red. It stood out amongst the trees like a beacon. If something went wrong, Samantha figured the rescue helicopters could at least spot the ugly paint job several miles away.

"It's going to feel so good to stretch my legs," Samantha said as they came to a stop. Tyler agreed. Together, they climbed out of the car and stretched their legs as far as they would go. Samantha kissed her husband on the cheek and thanked him for getting them there safely. Then she made her way to the SUV as her family piled out.

Her father was out first, stretching his arms above his head. He smiled at her and gave her hug. "Nice place, isn't it sweetie?" She nodded in agreement. Her mother, brother, and younger sister climbed out of the vehicle soon after and looked around.

"Kind of ugly, isn't it?" Ashley said.

"I think it gives it character," said Helen.

"That's what you call ugly things, Mom," Ashley stated. "You say the yappy little dog next door has 'character' and that thing is dumb and ugly."

Helen let out a smile that seemed to say *you got me* and helped her husband with the bags. Tyler and Samantha began to unload their car as well. Once all the bags were gathered up, they proceeded towards the front door. Tyler made his way to the front and gripped the lockbox on the doorknob. The lady he had rented the cabin from had given him the combination that same day over the phone. It had been easy to remember, but he wrote it down just in case. There would be spotty if any, cell service where they were staying. Calling to confirm the combination would be near impossible.

He pressed the numbers on the keypad and the panel slid open. Snatching up the silver key, he pressed it into the keyhole. "Everyone ready to go inside?" He asked. Without waiting for a response, he turned the key and pushed the door open.

II The Country Home

Tyler had rented the country home for the week as a gift to his in-laws. It was the first time they had ever been camping, though Tyler didn't really consider this camping. Tyler loved spending a lot of his time outdoors, mostly kayaking as often as he could. More specifically, kayaking through whitewater rapids. It was a thrilling experience that he hoped to one-day share with his wife, Samantha.

He had introduced her to kayaking and she fell in love with it immediately. But going through the rapids made her too nervous. Samantha promised to try one day and Tyler thought it best to not rush her. She would try it in time if she really wanted to. If not, he would be alright in Stillwater with her.

"Wow," Helen said. "This place sure is rustic." They looked around the cabin. Inside looked like a well-furnished home. There were two couches and a rocking chair circled around a fireplace in the living room. There was no television set anywhere in the country home, which was for the best. They were out there to enjoy nature, not watch mindless shows.

A sliding glass door next to the kitchen led to a wraparound porch covered in screen. Several rocking chairs sat on the wooden porch overlooking a magnificent sight. Trees stretched on forever in every direction. A wide river cut through the backyard and snaked its way through the trees. A small shack for the kayaks stood next to the soft churning water of the river.

Even though Tyler paid for the cabin, he opted to let Helen and Dan have the master bedroom. It was the largest room in the cabin with its own private restroom. At first, they had declined the nice offer but in the end, they had caved. Samantha and Tyler found their room at the end of a short hallway next to the bathroom. Ashley hurried behind them and picked the room right across the hall. Wesley was stuck with the room at the end of the hall.

Tyler and Samantha could hear Wesley gripe about his room in the distance. He had received the smallest of the three bedrooms. No furniture except a small bed sat inside and only one small window. It looked more like a prison cell than a bedroom. Tyler and Samantha would have switched with him if the bed had been bigger.

Instead, they settled into the room with a queen size bed, two picture windows, and an oak wood dresser with a solid mirror on top. It faced the bed on the opposite wall. Samantha looked over at it and then at the bed. "Thinking what I'm thinking?" She asked with a wink. He nodded and slipped a hand under her shirt and caressed her breast. Ashley stepped out of her room and the two of them pulled apart. It was like being teenagers at home with her family again. They smiled at each other and continued to put away their things.

When the family was done unpacking, they met around the fireplace and took a tour of the cabin. Slipping out of the sliding glass door, they checked out the wrap around porch. The rocking chairs looked comfortable and would be a great place to enjoy a morning coffee before the sunrise.

A few yards away from the cabin sat the fire ring. It was nothing more than a circle of rocks that formed a large pit but would work nicely. A large stack of firewood stood nearby, nearly the size of a small car. Samantha had a feeling they would get a nice fire going that night.

After unlocking the shed and seeing the kayaks and gear, the family headed back in the house to get started on dinner. They wanted to have dinner before the sunset and they knew it would happen fast. "Would you help me bring in the cooler?" Dan asked Tyler. He said he would and the two men headed out to the SUV.

When they got there, Dan opened the back and stopped. "Hey, I just wanted to say thanks, you know, for renting this place. It was a great idea. A nice family trip is exactly what we all need I think."

"Of course, Dan. Don't mention it. I love spending time with you guys. I couldn't think of anything better than to come out here and get some real quality time."

Dan smiled and reached in for the cooler. With that, the two men carried it inside and began to stock the fridge. Bending over to pull the bacon from the cooler, Dan said, "So, this kayaking trip you got us on tomorrow. You sure you mapped out the safest route?"

Tyler smiled.

"Yeah, I did my homework. There's a split in the river a few miles down. I marked it on the map. If we follow my path we'll be perfectly fine."

"Well, I'll trust your judgment."

"No worries, Dan. I've been doing this a while. Everything will be just fine. Promise."

Dan smiled and nodded as they loaded the last bit of food and drink into the fridge. He looked back up at Tyler and said, "Alright, dry cooler?" The two men shared a laugh and headed back out to the SUV.

Samantha and Helen began to pull food from the fridge to get a head start on cooking. As they did, they talked about their lives and current events. Samantha told her mother all about Tyler's business and how well it was doing. It allowed them to live a well and lavish life. Helen could not be happier for her daughter. All she had ever wanted was a good life for her kids. She and Dan had never been wealthy, though not quite poor either. But, wonderful trips like the one they were on were not something they had done often. She was grateful for Tyler's generosity to pay for the trip and bring their family together.

Tyler, Dan, Samantha, and Helen worked in the kitchen while Wesley and Ashley sat in their rooms. Eventually, dinner was ready and they sat around the large oak table as a family and consumed the delicious meal of steak, potatoes, and corn. With their stomachs full, the family sat on the porch and left the dishes to be cleaned up later.

The sun was beginning to set and Tyler suggested they make a fire in the fire pit soon. "You can't go camping without a fire," he said. Pulling himself out of the rocking chair, Tyler headed outside and down towards the pit with a flashlight in his hand.

Ashley got up and followed after him, telling everyone else she would help him start the fire. The rest of the family decided they would stay on the porch until the blaze was lit.

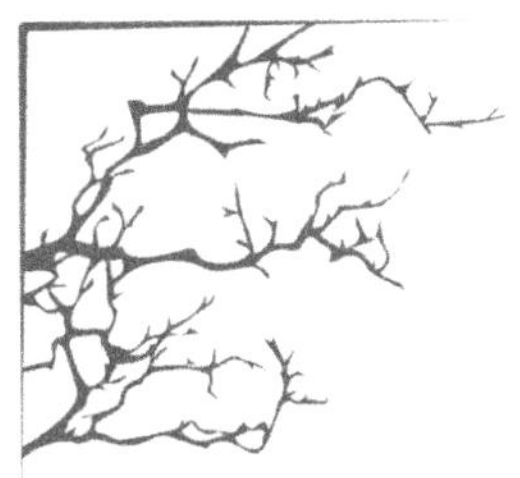

III The Fire

"**The trick** to starting a good campfire is to build it properly," Tyler said. Ashley looked over at him and smiled.

"Sounds like you've done this before."

"Maybe once or twice."

Ashley laughed.

He gathered up as many dead sticks as he could find and began to work on the fire. First, he built a small tipi shape using the smaller twigs with dead leaves inside. Once he was sure it was structured properly, he used the larger sticks to build a larger tipi around it.

"Shouldn't we smother the thing in gas or something?"

Tyler chuckled. "No," he said. "A good fire doesn't need to be started with lighter fluid. We should be able to get this thing burning bright with this alone." He held up a plain Bic lighter and smiled. Ashley smiled back at him and sat on the bench near the pit. Her flowing, satin shirt slid down and exposed her shoulders. She didn't bother to fix them. Instead, she ruffled her brown hair and stared at him. She hoped he would notice her but he was too fixated on the fire.

Leaning forward, she knew her cleavage would draw his attention. It was something she was well endowed with and usually got her the attention she wanted. Ashley had found Tyler attractive the day Samantha had brought him home to meet the family. He was a tall and slender man who kept himself well trimmed and clean. But he wasn't afraid to let his manly side show. Even now, he got himself dirty while building the fire and yet somehow it made him more attractive.

She had had dreams about him many times, not usually innocent. Ashley felt terrible for having these feelings about her sister's husband, but she could not help it. She had no intentions of stealing him away from her or wrecking their life. But if he wanted to have a taste of her, she wouldn't say no. If it ever happened, she was sure it would be a one-time-only thing.

Shame began to set in for trying to make her brother-in-law hit on her and she sat up. Tyler reached down and set the kindling on fire in the center of the tipi. After several seconds, the small spark turned into a roaring fire. The blaze engulfed the tipi and after a few minutes, it was burning brightly on its own with little help from Tyler.

"Nice going," Ashley said as she stood up and warmed her bare legs by the fire. She wasn't sure, but she thought she caught a glimpse of Tyler eyeing her smooth legs in the firelight. Turning her head away, she smiled. Maybe it would happen after all. She blushed, part from excitement and part from shame.

"How are things going with you?" He asked as he sat down on the opposite side of the fire. She rubbed the heat from her legs and sat back down. Fixing her disheveled hair, she looked over at him.

"Fine, I guess. My boyfriend left me a few weeks ago."

"Yeah, Samantha told me about that. Sorry to hear it."

"No big deal, really. Not the first time." The corner of her mouth twitched slightly and she barely took notice of it.

"His loss, right?"

"Exactly," she said and smiled at him.

"Well, life goes on. You'll find someone who appreciates you. I'm sure of it."

"Thanks," she said and flashed him a smile.

Smoke billowed from the fire and trailed its way over to Ashley. She waved her hand in front of her face and tried to lean out of the cloud. When it seemed like it was following her back and forth, she stood up and walked around the fire. Sitting next to Tyler, she said, "That's better."

Tyler laughed. "Hate it when smoke does that. Always seems like it is bothering you on purpose."

"Well, this is better seat anyway," she said pointing straight ahead. "The view is much better from here. The trees, the river, it's amazing."

Tyler said he agreed and the two of them sat in silence for a few moments. Ashley grabbed a large stick from nearby and poked at the fire. It continued to roar, casting dancing shadows on their faces. Ashley wiped the hair out of her eyes and leaned forward. Her shirt lifted and there was a noticeable draft on her lower back. She decided to ignore it.

STANDING AT THE kitchen sink, Samantha stared out the window. She had been in the middle of washing the dishes when she spotted her husband and sister out by the fire. She was glad they were getting along so well. But she could not help but feel a sting of jealousy. Her sister was beautiful. Samantha had always felt Ashley was far more beautiful than her. Not to mention she was younger. Shame set in as she realized it was her sister. Ashley would never try and take her husband away from her.

Then, she saw Ashley move from one side of the campfire to the other. Now, she sat next to Tyler. Samantha thought it was odd. There seemed to be no reason for the switch. She tried to shake off the growing feeling of jealousy until she watched her sister lean forward. For a moment, Tyler looked down and examined her lower back. Now, she felt real jealousy and fought back tears. There was no way the two of them were flirting with each other. But the idea started to drive her mad. She wondered what Tyler would do if Ashley threw herself at him.

She realized she was gripping a kitchen knife in her hand tighter than she meant to. Looking down at her shaking hand, she placed it back in the sink. "Hey," she said to her family. Her mother and father still sat at the table finishing their drinks, while her brother lay on the couch. "It looks like Tyler has a nice fire going. Want to go out there?"

"Of course," Dan said. "Let's check it out."

He and Helen stood up and stepped outside. Samantha called for Wesley to get up off the couch and he whined. "Do I have to go out there, too?" He said, pretending to be annoyed. Samantha told him he did and the two of them headed out the door, joining the family.

Ashley changed seats when Samantha came out. Samantha did her best not to give her a dirty look. Now she was sure she had been hitting on Tyler. She tried to tell herself it was because her relationship had recently ended. Ashley was in a bad place and was looking for any sort of relationship. She saw how happy she and Tyler were and it attracted her. Regardless, she still couldn't stand the thought of her sister trying to seduce her husband.

Shaking off the feeling, she tried to forget about it. The family enjoyed their time around the fire and talked. Tyler talked about his job, cluing the family in on a lot of what he did. Helen and Dan were extremely fascinated, or at least they acted like it. When Tyler came along, they got excited. When he started to pay for things, they were happier. Tyler had asked Samantha on more than one occasion if they only liked him because of the money. "Of course not," she would tell him. "They love and appreciate that you pay for as much as you do, I won't lie. But they would like you all the same." It always seemed to calm his worries.

Truth was, she wasn't always sure if her parents really liked him or just liked the money. They seemed to give him a lot of attention when he was around. Sometimes it bordered on brown nosing. But she had to believe they really did like Tyler for who he was, not how much he made. After all, she did.

For several more hours, they sat by the fire, making smores, enjoying small talk, and soaking in their surroundings. Ashley looked over at Tyler and said, "So, this kayaking trip tomorrow. Is it going to be safe?"

Tyler nodded and smiled.

"Yeah, it will be perfectly fine. I was telling Dan about it earlier. I've got the route all mapped out. Everything will go fine. Promise."

She nodded and stared back at the fire. Wesley looked up from the fire and over at Tyler. "What do we do if we happen to hit rapids?"

"Well, like I said, I mapped it out already. We shouldn't run into any rapids. But, if for some reason we do, don't panic. I know it sounds cliché, but don't. If you do capsize, float on your back with your feet pointing down river. It will reduce the risk of head injury on rocks. Once the water calms down, swim to shore. It wouldn't be too hard to find your way back here. You'd just follow the river. But everything will be fine, promise."

It seemed to put the whole family at ease. Samantha wasn't worried. She had been on several kayaking trips with Tyler. They had run into small rapids before and he was always able to handle them. They would be just fine.

She started to yawn and Helen followed suit. "Yeah," Dan stated. "I think it's about that time. We've got an early morning ahead of us."

"Agreed," Tyler said, standing up and inching towards the fire. "You guys go ahead inside. I'm going to make sure the fire gets put out."

"I'll meet you inside, sweetheart." Samantha kissed him and followed her mom inside. Wesley and Dan walked back towards the country home next. Ashley walked over to Tyler and asked if he would like any help with the fire.

"Not really. I can put it out pretty easy. It's getting pretty close to becoming nothing but embers anyway. But you're more than welcome to keep me company if you'd like."

She said she would and the two of them stayed up by the embers for another twenty minutes, filling the time with random chit chat. Finally, Ashley looked up at the night sky, seeing the bright burning stars. "They're so beautiful," she said, pointing. Tyler nodded.

"That one right there, the big bright one that has a sort of reddish hue." He said.

"Yeah?"

"It's actually Mars."

"No way. Really?"

"Yep. And I think Venus is out here as well."

He scanned the night sky until he found another bright star. This one was slightly bigger and brighter than the others.

"Ah, yeah there it is. See it?" He said pointing.

"Yeah."

"Venus is actually named after the Roman Goddess of beauty and love."

She looked over at him and gave him a smile. It glowed with the fire and starlight. Tyler found it to be slightly intoxicating. He never really noticed it before, but her smile was stunning. Though she was still looking up at the night sky, Tyler found himself staring at her. Shaking it off, he looked down at the fire.

"Looks like it's about to go out."

"I guess you're right. Thanks for the astronomy lesson. We should do it again later this week."

He smiled. "Sure. That would be fun."

With that, he snuffed out the fire and the two of them headed back inside.

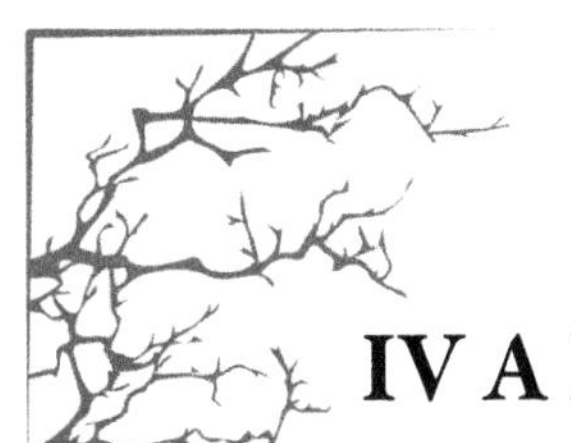

IV A Figure in the Trees

"**Hey, babe**," Samantha said from under the covers as Tyler stepped inside their room. "I was starting to wonder if you were ever coming in."

"Sorry, honey. I was making sure the embers didn't relight. Your sister stayed out there with me for a little bit and we got talking."

"That so? What about?"

"She went on about college, mostly. Seems like she's got a good future ahead of her. I feel bad about her boyfriend."

Samantha shrugged.

"Ashley's always had a difficult time holding on to a boyfriend."

"Shame."

Samantha nodded and watched her husband take off his shirt and pants. Still wearing his boxers, he started to climb into bed. "Wait a minute," she said. He watched as she slowly slid the blanket off her body. Like a magician pulling back a curtain, she revealed her beautiful body clad in black lingerie. It hugged her body nicely and begged for him to take her. He was instantly aroused and Samantha took notice. Wrapping her arms around his waist, she slid his boxers off.

After several minutes of kissing and caressing, the couple made love. It was passionate and wonderful, though they had to keep as silent as they could. The two of them giggled like teenagers hiding from their parents.

Finished, Tyler rolled off his wife and cuddled up next to her. He pulled her in tight against his naked flesh and smelled her hair. He could not help himself. He loved everything about her. Their moment of passion had painted a mile-wide smile on his face.

"Thank you, that was amazing," he said and kissed her on the lips.

"Likewise."

Tyler got up and switched off the lamp, flooding the room in total darkness. He crawled back in bed with his wife and pressed his naked body up against hers. She wiggled her hips to tease him and he seriously considered a second round drifting off to sleep.

He woke with a start and stared into the darkness. There was no alarm clock in the room and his phone was on the dresser far out of reach. Wanting to know what time it was, Tyler climbed out of bed and snatched up his phone. It was only half past two in the morning. Too early to stay awake and get started on the next day.

His bladder felt full and he decided to make a quick run to the bathroom. Figuring no one else would be up at this time, he decided to slip into the bathroom without putting on his clothes. It was risky but somehow gave him a thrill.

After relieving himself, he decided to head towards the kitchen. Comfortable that no one else would be awake, he continued to stroll around in the nude. There he grabbed a bottle of water out of the fridge and drank it down. Staring out the kitchen window, he enjoyed the night scene. The moonlight shone down on the forest, bouncing off the slowly flowing river. Tyler found something absolutely peaceful about the woods at night.

Leaning against the sink, now forgetting he was still naked, he stared at the tree line. There was a small clearing behind the house but the perimeter was surrounded by a thick tree line. He was on the lookout for any wild animals when he saw a shadow slip between the trees. Wondering if he had seen a deer or maybe a bear, he stared at the tree. A whole minute went by and nothing moved. He was starting to think he had been seeing things when a tall figure stepped out from behind the tree. Tyler was confused for a moment, unable to place what kind of animal it was. It was tall and thin and looked to be standing on two legs. He knew bears could sometimes stand up on their hind legs, but they were usually bulkier than the dark figure.

Whatever it was, it didn't seem to move. It was then Tyler realized it was looking in his direction. The full realization set in and his heart began to race. He was looking at a human being, most likely a man. He was just standing there in the woods, staring at the country home. "What the fu-"He was cut off by the sound of feet shuffling behind him.

His heart raced so fast he thought it might explode. He spun around and almost yelled in terror. Standing there staring at him in confusion was Ashley. "Tyler, what the hell are you- are you nake-"

"Ashley, look outside, quick." He spun around and pointed at the trees. Ashley walked up next to him and stared out the window. "Wait, there's nothing there now. I swear, there was something there before. It looked like a man."

"A man? All the way out here?"

"Yes. I swear to God I saw it."

"Maybe you saw an animal. Maybe a bear?"

"I don't know. I've seen a bear before. That didn't look like one."

"I doubt it was a person, Tyler. There aren't any other people out here for miles. But, there's a more pressing matter at hand."

"What?" He said, his chest heaving up and down with adrenaline and fear.

"I can see your dick."

Suddenly, he was filled with embarrassment. He had been so terrified with what he had seen, what he *thought* he had seen, that he forgot he was naked. Quickly, he cupped his hand around his crotch and apologized profusely. "Oh my god, I'm so sorry. This is, um, geez."

Ashley giggled and took a step towards him. It was then he realized she was only wearing a tee shirt and panties. An odd feeling of arousal stirred inside of him but he did his best to quiet it down. "It's alright,

Tyler. I don't mind." Tyler backed up and felt his bare butt press against the cold tile of the kitchen counter. He jumped a little at it.

"Let me just go get some-"

Ashley cut him off.

"You don't have to put anything on for me. I'd actually prefer if you didn't."

Tyler started to blush now. He had always thought of Samantha's sister as a beautiful woman. Over the years, he had had a few sexual dreams about her but always shook them off the next morning. She was attractive, yes, but he could never see himself sleeping with Ashley. He loved his wife. But a new feeling he had never felt before was sinking in. He could feel himself rising under his cupped hands. Ashley was inches away from him now. He could feel her breath on his chest.

"A-Ashley," he said, stumbling over her name. "I really should get back to-"

She interrupted him again but this time by pressing her lips hard against his. He tried to back away and bumped into the sink once again. Ashley pressed herself against him and slowly pulled his hands away from his body. Now there was no hiding his feelings. Ashley pulled away from him and looked down. "Gonna tell me you don't want this?" Wrapping her hands around his member, she led him to her room.

Samantha woke in the middle of the night and rolled over to kiss Tyler on the forehead. When she saw the bed was empty, she figured he must have got up to use the bathroom. Shutting her eyes, she waited for him to return. After a few minutes, she got out of bed and slipped on a dress.

Making her way into the hall, she headed for the bathroom. The door was wide open and Tyler was nowhere to be seen. Her next thought was that he had gone for a late-night walk. It was something he had done a few times before. Being a nature lover, it wasn't out of the question. She checked the sliding glass door which led to the back porch. It was locked. The front door was locked as well. It was clear he wasn't outside.

Having no idea where her husband could be, she headed back towards their room. She stopped at Ashley's room and thought about knocking on her door. She would feel terrible waking her, but she was getting worried. Raising her hand, she stopped short of knocking. Instead, she pressed her ear to the wooden door. Samantha heard the creak of bedsprings and soft moaning coming from inside.

Stumbling backward, she nearly fell to the floor. Turning around, she flung herself into her bed and cried into her pillow. Anger boiled inside of her but she did her best to repress it. Instead, she balled like a baby for a long while. She had been right to be jealous. Her husband was having an affair with her sister. Samantha was devastated and wondered how long it had been going on.

When the tears finally stopped flowing, the anger replaced sorrow. She balled her hands into fists and squeezed as hard as she could until her nails pierced the skin on her palms. A little blood trickled down and she paid it no mind. Instead, she only thought of how to get back at her husband. How would she confront him about it? How would she tell him she knew about their affair? Question after question rattled around in her mind when the door creaked open slowly.

Samantha went stiff and shut her eyes. Pretending to be asleep, she felt Tyler crawl into bed with her. His erect penis brushed against her and she fought the urge to turn around and tear it from his body. Instead, she pretended to wake from her slumber and rolled over. She looked into her husband's eyes and felt sickness and anger.

"Where'd you go?" She said, doing her best to sound half asleep.

"Had to go to the bathroom. Didn't mean to wake you."

Fucking shit head. You cheating little prick! She thought.

"It's OK."

With that, she rolled over again and the tears rolled down her cheeks. Silently, she cried until she drifted off to sleep. Her last thought before the darkness came was of hurting her husband. After all, he deserved it.

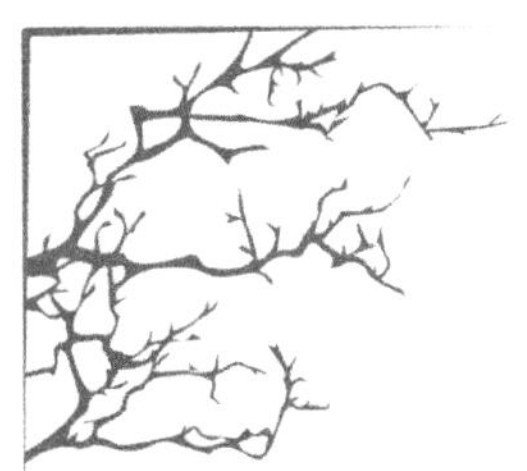

V His Secret

The morning dawn broke over the trees and the light poured into the bedroom windows. Tyler stared at the wall from the bed, having not slept since crawling back in. A few minutes after leaving Ashley's room, he had felt more remorse than he had ever felt in his life. Sexual desire had blinded him and urged him to do something utterly foolish.

After their affair, she had kissed him hard on the lips, thanked him, and told him to go back to bed and pretend nothing ever happened. But after seeing his wife's face in bed, he was filled with dread and despair. He had been unfaithful to her. Tyler loved his wife and he had cheated, with her sister no less. It was terrible. He *felt* terrible.

All night he had stayed up and cried. There was no chance of sleeping. What he had done was unforgivable. He would have to tell her the truth, no matter what it meant. He could not keep this from her. He had to come clean.

It was obvious Ashley did not really have feelings for him. There was a void in her that she needed to be filled. He had been her rebound. Someone she could easily be with and forget. She had never shown signs of interest in him before and he was sure things were no different. Regardless, it did not change what he had done. He decided he would tell her the truth after the trip was over. His lust would not ruin their entire trip. It would most likely destroy their relationship, but at least he'd be able to live with himself. This would be their last family trip, so he would make sure it was a memorable one.

Tyler sat up in bed and looked over at his wife. She seemed to be sleeping peacefully. Not wanting to disturb her, he slipped out of bed and got dressed. He wanted nothing more than to take a shower and wash the evidence of his affair from his body.

He stepped into the hallway and nearly bumped into none other than Ashley. Quickly shutting the bedroom door, Tyler said, "Hey, sorry." She smiled at him and shrugged.

"Nothing to be sorry about." She flashed a toothy smile at him and brushed past, making sure to graze up against him. He felt the familiar bustle of feelings inside before he forced them away. Grabbing her by the wrist, he led her to the living room.

"Look, Ashley. Last night was a mistake. I cheated on your sister. It's terrible and I can't forgive myself for that. It can't ever happen again. You understand? I love your sister and I want to make a life with her. I think I fucked all of that up last night."

"You sure as hell fucked something last night," she said with a wink.

"I'm not joking, Ashley. I messed up. How could we do that to Samantha? How could we do what we did last night? It was wrong."

"Ah, but it felt so good. I can still feel you, you know. I was hoping for another round later tonight. Maybe we could go out to the shed and-"

"No, Ashley, I can't. What is wrong with you? Why are you doing this?"

"Oh please, you enjoyed last night. I've seen the way you've looked at me. You've wanted this, you always have. Besides, my sister had it coming."

"What are you talking about? How did she deserve that?"

"Because she fucked my boyfriend."

Tyler nearly fell to the floor in astonishment.

"Wh-what did you say?"

"You heard me. Samantha slept with my boyfriend. She ruined our relationship. She said she was going to tell you about it but clearly, she lied. Everything we did last night, that was payback. That's not to say I didn't enjoy it, though."

"When did this happen? You're making this up, you have to be."

She shook her head.

"I'm not. It was before you two were married. It was the night of your bachelor party in fact. She had been telling me she was getting nervous, you know, cold feet. I told her there was nothing to worry about, that she had herself a wonderful and attractive man. You were, *are,* a catch. She acted as if she felt better. That night, I saw her riding my boyfriend. They don't know I saw them. I was supposed to be out with friends, but I had come home early. I don't know how long this has been going on with the two of them or if it had been a one-time thing, but regardless, they did it. I had to get back at her. Plus, I kinda always thought you were hot. Win-win, right?"

Tyler sat down on the couch and wiped a tear from his eye. His wife had been unfaithful. She had slept with a man only a few days before their wedding. How could she have done something like that? How dare she betray his trust? The thought sickened him and made him glad for his actions last night. In that moment, he wanted to sleep with Ashley again.

"I'm so sorry to tell you this. But I can't have you believing you're the one who ruined the relationship. It was her. She doesn't appreciate you like I do. She wouldn't do the things to you that I did last night. She's wrong for you. She's done wrong to you. You deserve better. I know that's my sister I'm talking about, but it's true. We can pretend what happened last night didn't, but I think we should keep it going. I think we should get back at her by sleeping behind her back. Let her think she got away with it."

She stepped closer.

"Let her think she won. Let her think there are no consequences to her actions. Meanwhile, you and I get to have all the fun. Think about it."

She gave him a wink and shoved her tongue down his throat. He caressed her cheek as they kissed. Once she pulled away, they both heard feet shuffle down the hallway. Ashley spun around to see her sister come around the corner. Samantha stopped when she spotted the two of them standing there.

"Morning, sis," Ashley said as she walked towards the kitchen. "Tyler was just telling me a little about our kayak trip today. Sounds like it should be a lot of fun. Maybe a little rough riding, but should be nice."

Tyler thought he saw his wife shudder but couldn't be sure. Now, he was filled with a sort of disgust with her. Knowing she had let another man inside of her while she was supposed to be faithful to him was disgusting. He wanted nothing to do with her.

"Morning, babe." He said, trying not to grit his teeth. "Sorry I didn't wake you. I figured you'd want to get your sleep."

"Thanks," she said and sat on the couch. Tyler decided to sit outside on the porch and left the two ladies in the house. Soon, the rest of the family started to stir. Within minutes, breakfast was underway.

The family ate around the table but Samantha and Tyler were not very talkative. Dan and Helen inquired about it, but both responded they had not slept very well. To which Ashley said, "I slept great last night. Felt great." Samantha dropped her fork and it clattered to the ground.

"Let me get you a new fork, honey," Helen said and grabbed one from the kitchen. She thanked her mom and went back to eating her eggs.

They mostly ate in silence after that, no one really having anything particular to say. It was as if everyone could read the tension in the room. When they were done, the plates were cleared off and washed. Shortly after, Wesley and Dan took a walk down to the shed to check on the kayaks. Helen and Ashley got to work packing some bags of items they would bring with them on the excursion.

Samantha went into the bedroom and started to pack a bag of her own and stopped. Tyler stepped into the room and saw her standing there, arms at her sides. "Something wrong?" He asked her. She shook her head and shrugged.

"I don't know, maybe. I just had a really bad dream last night, that's all."

"Is that so? What about?" He asked her but really did not care. After what he had learned, she could have been on fire and he wouldn't piss on her to save her life. Again, she shrugged.

"I don't really remember I guess."

He shrugged and helped her pack a bag. They're hands brushed together and she stopped moving. "You know what, I don't think I'm feeling that good. Must be I didn't sleep very well. I don't think I should go on the trip today. Maybe later this week."

Something was up with his wife and he could not figure out what it was. Maybe she had seen them last night. Maybe she knew what he had done. He would have cared if it wasn't for learning she had slept with another man first. He decided he wanted to get to the bottom of it all and tell her he knew about her affair.

"You know what, I'm glad you said it. I don't feel good either. I didn't want to be the only one to stay back. But I'll stay back with you. We could have a little *fun* together here." Something about the way he pronounced the word fun made his own skin crawl, though he could not figure out what it was.

"Ok." She said, half asking, half stating. He couldn't figure out if she were happy or miserable he was staying. Deciding he didn't care, he left the room.

Dan and Wesley came back in the house and sat at the table. "Kayaks are all pulled out and ready," Dan said. He looked over at Tyler. "You got the map?" Tyler nodded.

"I'll give you the map, actually. Samantha and I are going to stay back today. We really didn't sleep well."

"We can go kayaking a different day," Helen said from the kitchen. "We don't want to leave you two behind."

"It's fine, really. I think we just need to catch up on some sleep. You guys go ahead without us. We'll go again later this week. It'll be fine."

Convinced, the family said they would continue as planned and finished getting ready. Within thirty minutes, the family was settling in their kayaks and getting ready to launch down the river. "Remember," Tyler began. "Follow the map. It will take you away from the rapids." Wesley said they would and they started down the river, leaving Samantha and Tyler alone. They looked at each other and walked silently back to the country home.

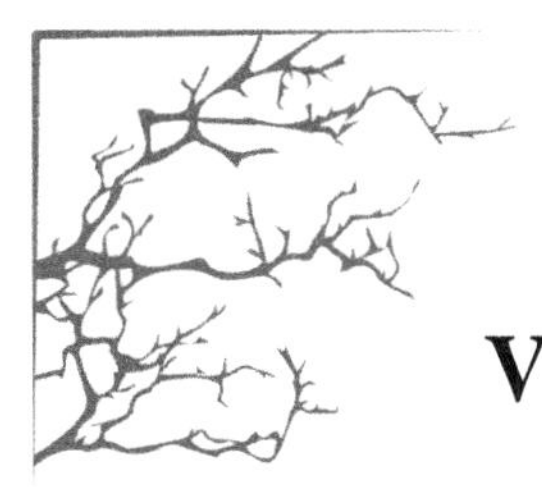

VI Confrontation

Despite knowing his wife had cheated on him first, Tyler could not help but feel awful about what he had done. He had done it without the knowledge of her infidelity. It did not make him right or wrong, it just *was.* He knew he had to come clean about the whole thing. There was no other choice. The two of them couldn't continue living in a lie.

Samantha silently walked through the country home and stumbled into their bedroom. Tyler could hear her flop down on the bed. Then he heard something he had not expected. Tears. *What the hell is she crying about?* He wondered. Did she feel bad about her affair? Was the guilt finally eating her up? Or was it something else?

Her crying grew louder as he made his way down the hallway. Hesitating for a single moment outside the door, he almost withdrew. Instead, he nudged the door open with his foot and stepped inside, knowing there was no backing out now.

"Samantha, I think we need to talk."

"Oh, you *think*?"

"I do. Something happened that I'm not proud of. I-"

Samantha sat up in the bed and craned her neck towards him.

"You fucked my sister? Yeah, I know."

"Samantha, I can-"

"You know what? Save it. I don't care what explanation you have. You were drunk, you were horny, I didn't give you enough attention, your father didn't show you enough love as a child. It doesn't fucking matter. You cheated on me, Tyler. You can't justify it with anything."

"Yeah, but you-"

"No! You shut your disgusting mouth!" She screamed. "You're a disgusting piece of shit. You *fucked* my sister. Who does that? If you wanted pussy, why not a random chick at a bar or a co-worker. Why my sister? *Why?*"

"It didn't happen like that. I didn't go to-"

"I said I don't care. I'm done with you. Cheating isn't something we can come back from. And cheating with my sister. Well, you're lucky I don't stab you in the God damned throat!"

Anger welled up inside of Tyler now. He knew he was wrong for sleeping with her sister but what she had done was just as bad. Now was the time for her to pay for her sins.

"Oh, you think you're so high and mighty, do you? You think that you're better than me? Yes, your sister seduced me last night, I was weak. But at least I didn't fuck her boyfriend." He nearly yelled.

She looked up at him with pursed lips and tilted head. Her eyes darted around the room as if she were looking for something to say. Finally, she said, "What the *hell* are you talking about?"

"Oh, you know damn well what I'm talking about. You slept with Ashley's boyfriend the night of my bachelor party."

"I have no ide-"

"Don't give me your lies. Ashley saw you two. She said you were riding him pretty hard. Clearly, you were having a good time. I didn't even have a stripper at my party because I was thinking of you too much. And there you were riding some other guy. So, don't sit there and talk to me like I made the mistake. You made it first. I'm glad I slept with your sister. After what you did, you deserved it."

She stared at him, her mouth agape. Shaking her head as if she could not believe what she was hearing, she said, "Tyler, I didn't sleep with Ashley's boyfriend. I don't know what you're talking about."

"Sure, pretend you have no idea. Why hide it anymore? What, do you want to be the victim here, is that it? If you admit you slept with another man then I won't seem as bad?"

"No, I didn't-"

"I don't think so. If you're not going to tell me the truth then I don't want to hear you speak."

"Tyler, please." Tears started to roll down her face. "Believe me, I didn't do anything. Is that why you did it? Were you trying to get back at me? Because there is nothing to get back at me for."

Tyler was confused. Why would she deny sleeping with another man if she knew he had slept with her sister? It didn't seem to make sense. Unless...

"You wanted this to happen. You hoped Samantha would see you. You knew how conniving she could be and you hoped she would get me to sleep with her over it. That way you could have this whole relationship ended. It's your way out."

"No," she cried. "I love you so much, Tyler. I would never have betrayed you like that. You have to believe me. We can get past this, we can. I'm sorry you think I cheated on you. I'm sorry my sister lied to you. I don't know if I can get over you being with my sister but we can try. I want to try."

Tyler shook his head.

"*You* banged another man. Don't sit here and pretend it didn't happen. It makes no sense."

If she didn't want them to end, why was she lying? Tyler couldn't imagine it. He had admitted to sleeping with her sister. Why couldn't she admit what she had done? She only wanted Tyler to be the villain.

"Fuck this," he said. "If you're not going to admit it then I don't want to see your face."

He stormed out of the room and headed towards the porch. Without a second thought, he barged outside and headed towards the tree line. Samantha screamed for him to come back but never left her bed. When she heard him step off the porch, she cried once again.

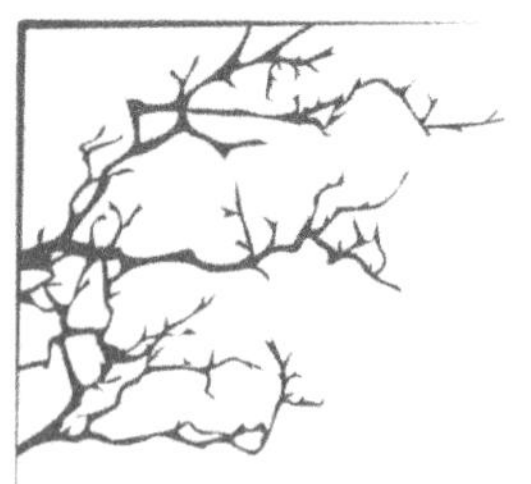

VII Rapids

Ashley was having a wonderful time on the calm and soothing waters of the river. Even Wesley, who was usually known for finding something wrong with nearly everything, seemed to be enjoying the journey. Helen and Dan rowed in rhythmic symmetry aboard their tandem kayak. Everyone smiled.

"I wish Tyler and Samantha were out here with us," Helen finally said. "It's too bad they didn't feel good."

Dan agreed as they continued on their way. As they passed a mud bank, an alligator dashed into the water and made Ashley scream. Afterwards, she giggled like a little girl. "That scared me," she said. Wesley looked at his sister and shook his head.

"I think you scared it."

"Oh yeah, like I'm so scary."

Wesley dipped his hand into the river and splashed his sister. She laughed and returned a hand-full of water. Helen and Dan smiled. It had always seemed the two were at each other throats. It was refreshing to see them happy together.

The relationship had degraded between the two siblings once they moved out of their parents' house. Their distance could be attributed to a myriad of disagreements but mostly it was politics. Ashley had taken on a more liberal view of the world around her while Wesley remained ever conservative. At least one Thanksgiving had been ruined by political squabble. Wesley had stormed out of the house in the middle of the meal and did not come back. Helen had cried that night, hoping her two kids would get along again. Now, a tear of joy rolled down her cheek. This was long overdue for their family.

"There's no way we can properly thank Tyler for all this," Dan said. "We've got to do something nice for him. He was nice enough to pay for this whole trip."

"Like what?" Wesley asked.

Dan shrugged.

"No idea. Let's talk about it when we're not rowing down a river."

"Looks like there's a fork in the river coming up, Dad," Wesley announced. "Left, or right? What's the map say?"

Dan ceased paddling and pulled the map out of his bag. A red line painted a path down the river to a big red X on the map. It marked the return vehicle Tyler had asked the owner of the cabin to leave for them.

"Tyler's mark goes left. He said he marked the map to keep us away from rapids. I guess we go that way." Dan said.

"Let's hope he knows how to read a map." Wesley joked.

"He does this all the time," Dan retorted. "I think we can trust him."

With that, they continued down the river towards the left branch. As they made the turn down the left branch, everything seemed fine. They continued to enjoy the trip. Eventually, Wesley said, "Uh, guys, did the river just get a little faster?"

"Now we don't have to paddle as hard," Ashley stated.

Wesley looked at his parents, a slight panic in his eyes. They seemed to pay it no mind. There was no reason not to believe him. Dan's face changed from confident to worried once the water began to become choppy.

"I see whitewater," Wesley said. "Doesn't that mean rapids?"

"Maybe it's normal for the river to get a little bumpy," Helen said. "Doesn't necessarily mean it's rapids."

Wesley looked down the river and his mouth dropped open. "I don't think *that's* normal," he said, pointing with his paddle. Up ahead, the water was foaming white and rushing at high speed around jagged rocks and fallen tree limbs. A portion of the roaring river dropped out of view making it impossible to tell how steep it was.

"What the hell do we do?" Ashley yelled.

"Head for the bank," Dan screamed. But the current was pulling them faster than they could manage. There was no escaping the rapids. Out in front, Wesley was the first to go over the ledge. The nose of the kayak dipped into the water and he flailed out his arms. The kayak tipped on its side and he slid out. Immediately, the current dragged him under the water.

"Wesley," Helen screamed. The kayak bobbed back to the surface for a moment before following Wesley down the river. To his parents' horror, it crashed against several of the razor-sharp rocks as it went. There was little time to worry, however, as the remainder of the family went over the ledge.

"Hang on," Dan yelled as they went over. Thankfully, none of them capsized. Struggling to keep her kayak straight, Ashley stuck her paddle in the rushing rapids. Her kayak shifted to the left and then spun completely around, causing her to traverse the rapids backward.

"Daddy, I can't see where I'm going."

Dan and Helen tried to paddle to her but the current was too strong. They banged against a rock and Helen went overboard. Dan screamed for her but there was nothing more he could do. He watched as she slammed against a rock and shot down river like a bullet from a gun.

The nose of his kayak wobbled left and right. Desperately, Dan tried to control it but it was no use. It would only be a matter of time before he went in as well. Ashley, still sitting upright, started to panic. Water splashed all around her, matting her hair to her body. With all of her strength, she tried to spin the kayak but nothing worked. Faintly, her dad's voice called out to her above the roar of the river.

The rapids carried them down river for miles. They smashed against rocks and nearly capsized several times. Somehow, Dan and Ashley were able to keep afloat. A fallen tree lay across half the river like a dam. It created an intense flow of water to its left. Dan spotted the branch and tried to steer the kayak towards the rush of whitewater.

To Dan's horror, the back end of her kayak smashed against the wet bark of a tree and the craft flipped up into the air. Ashley screamed as she dropped into the water, scraping against several tree branches as she did. Then, she was sucked away by the current. Her kayak smashed against a rock and splintered into pieces.

Only Dan remained upright now. He could only pray his family would make it through the rapids with minimal damage and end up in calmer waters. It felt like hours as he fought to keep above the churning water. Now, he had to worry about keeping himself safe. If he went under now, there might not be a chance to save his family later.

It didn't take long, however, for a jutting rock to capsize his kayak as well. A sharp piece cut through his shirt sleeve and into his flesh. Crying out in pain, he too slipped below the surface and was dragged down river.

VIII Calmer Waters

Gasping for air, Dan found himself floating in a calm section of the river. The faint roar of water in the distance assured him the danger was now over.

He swam to one side and climbed up the river bank. His feet sunk into the thick mud multiple times as he attempted to climb the bank. Both shoes were sucked from his feet, allowing Dan to pull free of the mud with a loud *plop!* Catching his breath, he sat on the grass and counted himself lucky to be alive.

A shiver of fear shot up his spine as he thought about the rest of the family. Wesley had been the first to go under and they had not seen him resurface. Wesley could have been trapped under a rock and drowned in the rushing water. The thought haunted Dan.

After Wesley, Helen had gone over. She had crashed against several rocks before being sucked down river. There was a chance she had found safety but he couldn't shake the fear she had been knocked unconscious and drowned.

Then there was Ashley. An image of her stuck in the branches of the tree and drowning burned into his mind. The thought of losing nearly his entire family made him nauseous. Dan leaned his palms against his knees and vomited. Wiping his mouth clean, he watched the calm waters of the river.

A twig crunched somewhere nearby and Dan sprang back to life. A few yards upriver, Dan spotted his wife clawing her way through the mud. "Oh, thank God," he cried aloud and ran to her. After pulling her free, he wrapped his arms tightly around her.

"Where are the kids?" She asked. Dan shook his head, still happy to see someone. "We need to find them, Dan."

"I know, sweetheart. We will. I think we need to check the riverbank to make sure neither of them washed up unconscious."

She nodded.

They decided to split up. Helen would head up river and Dan would patrol the opposite. They would only walk two hundred paces before turning back and meeting up again.

Dan walked his two hundred paces but found nothing. Refusing to give up, he walked a little more. After another few hundred paces, he found the tangled mess that was Ashley's kayak. He could only hope she had washed up somewhere nearby.

Sure enough, he found her lying on her back at the edge of the river. The water slowly lapped at her bare feet. Dan placed two fingers under her nose and rejoiced when he felt a stream of air. With a couple taps to the cheek, his daughter started to stir.

"Where am I?" She asked, rubbing the side of her head. "I feel like I got run over by a train. Jesus."

"It's OK, honey. You're safe now."

He gave her a big hug and helped her to her feet.

"Your mother's going to be happy to see you. Come on, let's meet up with her. Hopefully, she found Wesley."

Ashley and Dan met up with Helen. Even though Wesley had yet to be found, the family still took solace in a warm embrace together. "What do we do now?" Helen asked. Dan stared at the stagnant river for several minutes before making a decision.

"We can't just leave Wesley out here. If the rest of us ended up here, he can't be far away."

"What if he was swept further down river?" Ashley asked.

"Then we have to search for him before heading back, right?"

Helen nodded. There was no way they could try and find their way back to the country home without at least looking for Wesley. If he had been swept further down river, they might be able to stumble across him. More than likely, he would be following the river back towards the cabin and they would run into him.

"Wait, what if he didn't go as far as us," Helen said. "And he's further up river. He might start heading back before us and we'll miss him."

"Well, in that case, we'll meet up with him at the house eventually. If we stay out here and search for him and he's already back at home, no worries. If we decide to go back now and he's unconscious down river, well..."

He didn't have to finish his sentence. They all knew what it would mean. If Wesley was downriver, face stuck in the mud, he would need their help right away. But if he was already headed back to the house, there would be no problem waiting for him here or searching. They might waste a day in the woods, but it would be better to know Wesley was safe.

"When we're ready to head back, we can just follow the river," Dan said. "It shouldn't be too hard."

"We just don't know how far the river took us," Ashley stated.

She was right. When they had hit the rapids, they weren't awfully far from camp. But the rapids had carried on for what seemed an eternity. They could be miles away by now. It could take hours to get back, maybe even a day. There was no way of knowing.

"Should we split up?" Ashley wondered aloud. "Maybe I head back to the cabin and you two stay out here and look for Wesley."

"No, we need to stay together. We can't split up." Dan ordered.

"Dad, seriously, it's just up the river. You said so yourself. It wouldn't be that hard."

"And if something happens to you?"

"Like getting swept down river in the rapids? I think I can handle a simple walk, dad. You don't have to worry about me. Besides, maybe it would be best for someone to make it back home today and let Tyler and Samantha know what happened. When we don't show back up before sundown, they're going to worry. We can't have them out here looking for us. They would be wandering down river, the *wrong* part of the river no less. More of a chance for something to happen to them."

Dan rubbed the back of his head in frustration. His daughter was right. As much as he hated the thought, it would be a good idea for them to split up. He didn't want her going alone, though. He thought Helen should go with her. When he voiced his opinion, however, Ashley protested again.

"I'm afraid I agree with Ashley," Helen said. "As much as I hate to send her out there alone, she'll have the easier job. Following the river back home will be easier. If she leaves now, she could get back before sunset, assuming we're not too far gone. You're going to need all the help you can get out here. There's a lot of ground to cover. And what if Wesley needs help? One of us can stay with him while the other hauls ass back to camp. I really see no way around it."

Ashley smiled at her father. "Dad, I'll be just fine. I promise. Nothing can go wrong. I'll just be walking home. It'll be easy. Plus, I can keep an eye out for Wesley. What if he's unconscious farther upriver? He'll need help just the same."

He thought for several minutes, knowing there were no other options but he desperately wanted one. Finally, he approached his daughter and took her in his arms. "You be extra careful, OK. If something doesn't seem right, you follow the river back here. We'll find you. I don't want you taking any chances."

"Dad, I'm going to be fine. It's just upriver. There's no chainsaw wielding maniacs out here. I think I'll make it."

He rolled his eyes at her, knowing she was making fun of him. He kissed her on the cheek and said, "I love you, Ashley. Let Samantha and Tyler know we're safe. We'll be heading back as soon as we can."

She nodded and turned around. With that, she headed back up the river, her feet sliding in the mud only once until she was out of sight of her parents. Dan was still worried about her long after he could no longer see her. He prayed to God he would watch over her and keep her safe. Then he prayed Wesley would be found safe and sound.

IX Chasing Shadows

With an anger still in his gut, Tyler still crunched through the trees. It had been well over an hour since he had left the cabin and he wasn't quite sure where he was. It wouldn't be too hard to find his way back, though. He could still hear the sound of the river nearby. If he could find it, he would find home. He wasn't worried.

Besides, he couldn't fathom the thought of being under the same roof as his wife. She had had an affair some time ago and refused to admit it. Instead, she would rather lie and make it worse. It was obvious she never truly loved him. Maybe it was for the best. Maybe he never truly loved her.

Despite everything, he still could not help but have feelings for his wife. He tried to ignore it, but he found himself thinking about all the good times. All the fun they had ever had together. There had been many smiles in their relationship, many adventures. He couldn't picture himself throwing it all away. Now, he hoped they could get back to where they were. Maybe they could patch things up. Maybe he was willing to work on it.

But the thought of her lying about her affair resurfaced and he wasn't certain. His thoughts scattered in every direction like shrapnel from a grenade. He no longer knew how to feel. He no longer knew if he was mad at her or if he wanted to give it a chance. Neither seemed like a viable option.

Tyler decided it was best not to think about it anymore. He would deal with it when the time was right. Now, he needed to work on clearing his head. Being out in the wilderness was the best way to accomplish that. He had read articles which claimed a person's mind was more relaxed when experiencing nature and he believed it. Few problems in his life couldn't be solved after a nice walk through the woods.

He heard something brush through the trees and he stopped for a moment. It sounded big, maybe a bear. The memory of the dark figure lurking in the trees the night before came flooding back. Because of the ordeal with Ashley, he had forgotten all about it.

"Shit," he whispered, looking around. Whoever or whatever it was could be watching him now. Maybe it was hunting him. Maybe it wanted its prey to be alone so it could finally take him out. A million thoughts ran through his mind before he finally pushed them away. Ashley had looked out the window and saw nothing. It had to have been in his mind. Maybe it was just a shadow. But he knew that was not like him.

Tyler had never been the jumpy type. Whenever he heard a noise late in the night, he was quick to rationalize it. Never did he jump to silly conclusions like ax murderers or ghosts. Usually, the simplest explanation was the right one. In this case, it had to have been an animal. Maybe it was a deer grazing in the grass, standing up on its hind legs to grab at some berries.

Feeling slightly better, he heard something brush through the trees again. This time he realized it was too big to be an animal like a deer or raccoon. No, it was something bigger. It sounded like it walked on two legs. Tyler thought he could hear the methodic dual crunch on leaves like footsteps. Shortly after, it stopped.

Crouching down low, he snuck behind a tree and waited for the sound to come back. When it did, he was terrified to hear it had drawn closer. His blood ran ice cold as if his veins were filled with spring water. Crouched behind a tree, frozen in utter horror, he saw the outline of a man in the distance.

At least, he assumed it was a man. The figure was well hidden, a thick jacket draped over its shoulders and a hood around its head. Long baggy pants made it impossible to discern the size. Black gloves covered the hands. Tyler couldn't be sure, but it seemed the face was obscured by a piece of fabric as well.

Now it was official. Someone *had* been in the woods last night, watching him. Or at the very least, he had been watching the house. His mind told him to spring on the watcher. After all, he had the element of surprise. But fear kept him frozen in place.

When the figure moved farther away, Tyler slowly made his way back towards the river. Stopping, he checked all around to make sure nothing had followed. Before Tyler could breathe a sigh of relief, he spotted the watcher several yards behind, not moving a muscle. It seemed to stand unnaturally still. Not even the subtle upheaval of breath. The watcher merely stood there, staring at Tyler.

Heart thudding against his rib cage, Tyler ran as fast as his feet would carry him back towards the country home. When it finally materialized from the trees, he thought the peeling yellow paint was the most beautiful thing he had ever seen. He heard nothing behind him, having expected the distinct sound of footfalls as the watcher gave chase. Daring a glance over his shoulder, he saw he was completely alone. But it did nothing to calm his racing heart and slow his breakneck pace.

Bolting straight inside, he slammed the door as hard as he could. Samantha was lying on the couch, tears running down her face. Now, however, she sat upright and stared at her husband. "What in the hell are you doing?" She screamed at him.

"We need to lock this place down," he said.

"What? Why? Are you feeling-"

"Samantha, I'm not fucking joking. There's some guy out there."

"A guy? Like a hiker or something?"

"No hiker wears a thick ass jacket, face mask, and hood in the middle of summer in the god damned woods."

"Ok, OK, don't get so pissy."

"Get up. Help me make sure this place is locked."

“Wait a minute, Tyler. How do I know this is even real? Is this just some bullshit ploy to get me to talk to you? After what you did, I don't care what you have to say.”

“Samantha, I’m not fucking around here. There’s someone out there.”

“And? What did they do? Did they try and kill you? Was it Jason? Maybe Michael Myers?”

“No, but-“

“So, you saw a person, freaked out, and ran inside? For all you know, it could have been a guy lost in the woods and you ran screaming from him like a little bitch. Maybe I should go out there and find-“

“Absolutely not,” Tyler said, putting himself between her and the exit. “I can’t let you go out there. There’s something wrong with this guy, I’m telling you. Last night, I saw him standing in the trees just staring at the house.”

“Was that before or after you fucked my little sister.”

“Jesus Christ, Samantha. Something isn’t right here. Please, you have to believe me.”

She rolled her eyes.

“Fine, I’ll play your little fucking game. But if you’re lying to just get me to talk to you, I’m going to kick you so hard in the balls.”

“Jesus fucking Christ,” he yelled.

“What?” she nearly yelled back from the couch.

“He’s out there right now. He’s walking through the trees. I think he followed me back.”

“Let me see.”

Tyler pulled his glance away from the window long enough to watch Samantha lift off the couch and head his way. When Tyler turned back to the window, his draw dropped in horror. “Wait, what?” All Samantha saw were a couple of squirrels chasing each other up the bark of a tree.

"Are you feeling alright, Tyler? Did you hit your head out there? Or maybe it's hysteria. Sleeping with my sister caused you to go mad."

It made no sense. The man was there, he had seen him. There was no way he had vanished. Scratching his head, Tyler turned back towards his wife. Anger welled up in her eyes like a fiery pit.

"Maybe you're trying to scare me. Is that it?"

"No, I-"

"Scare me so you can keep me safe from the big scary man outside."

"It's not like that, Samantha. I swear to God."

"Go fuck yourself, Tyler," She said as she stomped back towards their room. She slammed the door and threw herself on the bed. Tyler could make out her sobs as he sat down on the couch, starting to question his own sanity. Something was very wrong with these woods. *Or,* he thought, putting his face in his hands, *there's something very wrong with me.*

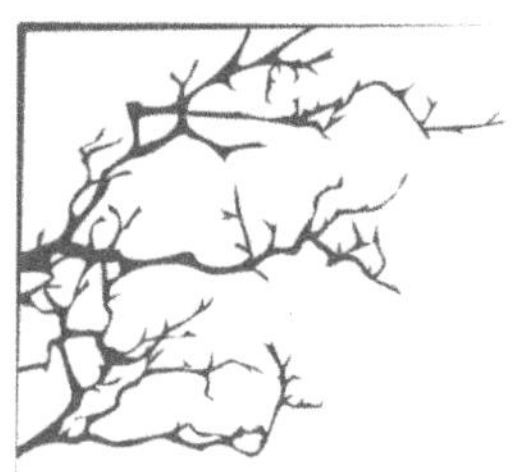

X Torment

Samantha lay on her bed, sobbing her eyes out. Tyler was not the man she had married, not anymore. Something seemed wrong. He had betrayed her and slept with her sister. And worse, he was trying to justify it with a story that was clearly bullshit. Samantha had no clue where he got the idea she had slept with Ashley's boyfriend. It was completely wrong. Now, he was ranting about seeing a man in the woods. She was beginning to fear for his mental health. Perhaps something had snapped inside his head.

It was ridiculous. Tyler had a good head on his shoulders, he always had. There was no way something was wrong with him, not out of nowhere like this. She couldn't believe it. But she had seen it for herself. It was like his personality had changed overnight. Before, he never would have entertained the idea of sleeping with another woman. It wasn't like him, none of this was.

She couldn't think of it any longer. A headache formed at her temples and she pressed on them in agony. Standing up from the bed, she heard Tyler at the door. "Sweetheart, please let me in. I don't want you to be alone right now. I'm telling you I saw something."

Rolling her eyes, Samantha said, "Drop it, Tyler. I'm not falling for your cheap games. I don't want to see you right now. Just looking at you makes my stomach churn."

She could hear him sigh and step away from the door. Without another word, he was gone. Something tugged at her heartstrings but she shook it away. There was no chance she was going to feel bad for a cheating, lying asshole. He deserved to be shunned. He deserved far worse than that. Samantha let an anger boil inside her. She would have smacked him until her arm went numb had he been in the room with her. Then, she would beat her sister senseless with the other.

Something scraped against the outside wall of the cabin, like a branch from a tree shaking in the wind. She knew there was a large tree that stood in the front yard but couldn't remember if it was close enough to touch the house. Assuming it was, she sat back down on the bed and looked at herself in the mirror. She looked terrible. Deep dark circles rested under her bloodshot eyes. Her hair was disheveled and matted against her face. *No wonder he cheated on me* she thought. *I'm such a mess.* Then she shook her head. *I look like this because of what he did to me.*

The scraping continued and carried on to the window. A rhythmic tapping ticked against the glass. She spun on her heel and looked at the curtain. "Was the tree close enough to tap the glass?" She said as she took a step towards the curtain and outstretched her arm.

Her fingers grazed the curtain but she let her arm fall to her side. Maybe it was just Tyler trying to get her attention. He couldn't get to her through the door and now he was trying at her window. No, she wasn't going to fall for it. Tyler needed to leave her alone and that was final.

"Give it a rest, Tyler. I don't want to see you right now."

The tapping continued, only louder.

"I said, I don't want to see you. Leave me alone."

Again, the tapping increased in intensity.

Not able to take it any longer, she stepped over to the window. In one swift movement, she flung open the curtains and nearly toppled to the floor. Samantha let out a blood-curdling scream that echoed through the halls of the cabin.

Tyler had heard Samantha scream and bolted to the bedroom door as fast as he could. Slamming his fist against it, he begged her to open the door. Fearing the worst, he tried to bash it in with his shoulder. He bounced off it and nearly toppled to the ground. As he reared back to try again, the door swung open and Samantha came running out, pushing past Tyler and heading straight for the living room.

She darted towards the front door and engaged the lock. Tyler begged her to tell her what was going on. She ignored him and continued to check the locks around the house. Once she seemed confident everything was secure, she dropped on the couch and took a deep breath.

"You saw him, didn't you?" Tyler asked. "See, I told you. I wasn't making it up."

"Jesus Christ, Tyler, I don't know what I saw. There was *something* outside my window. The moment I screamed, it was gone. I barely got a good look at it."

"Someone is out there. You have to believe me now."

Samantha shrugged.

"What do we do now?" She asked, sounding nervous.

Tyler had no idea. They needed help but there was no cell signal this far out. The country home had no landline phone either. There was a car out front. If they were fast enough, they might be able to hop in and drive off towards the safety of a nearby town. But that meant leaving Samantha's family behind. They would be coming home later that evening and would be incredibly unprepared. Tyler had a suspicion the masked man would not leave them alone, though he couldn't explain how he knew.

"We have to stay in here, fortify this place."

"What about getting help?"

"Can't. If we leave and your family comes back..."

He didn't bother finishing his sentence. They both knew exactly what he meant. Only, they had no idea what was going on. Whoever was out there had not attacked them yet. They could not be sure he was violent. Maybe he was a backwoods redneck who was a little slow in the head. Maybe he was just curious about the inhabitants of the country home. But Tyler had seen enough horror movies to know better.

"Alright, fine. We lock this place down. We make sure everything is barricaded so this freak can't get in here." Samantha said.

"Good plan. There's got to be some tools in the garage. Maybe there's even some sort of supplies in there."

"You check. I'm not going anywhere near it."

"What? Why?"

"Are you kidding me? Have you ever seen a horror movie?"

Tyler shook his head.

"Alright, fine. You stay in here. See what you can find in the kitchen or something. I'll be right back."

He hesitated for a moment, waiting to see if Samantha would protest. When she didn't, he turned around and headed for the door leading to the garage. Quietly, he pushed it open and stepped inside.

It was a dusty and cluttered place. A riding lawn mower sat in the middle of the concrete floor with a dirt-covered chest freezer behind it. Shelving units lined the walls with all kinds of junk strewn about. Old newspapers, rope, blocks of woods, and tools stuffed into corners.

Shuffling across the trash littered floor, Tyler made his way to one of the shelves. As he searched, looking for anything useful, he heard a *bang.* Spinning around, he realized the door leading outside was wide open. It danced in the wind like the branch of a tree, tapping against the outside wall.

He scanned the room but saw nothing out of the ordinary. He shuffled his feet towards the door. Halfway there he froze. A reflection glimmered in the window of the open door. At first, he had thought it was his reflection but upon closer inspection, he realized it was the cloaked figure in the room behind him.

Terror struck and his heart raced wildly in his chest. Desperately, he tried to think of something to use as a weapon. Taking his eyes from the window, he scanned the shelving unit next to the door. He spotted a ball peen hammer and lunged for it. With one quick motion, he turned to face his would-be assailant. To his surprise, they were gone.

"What the fuck?" He asked himself.

It was impossible. He had just seen the reflection in the window, he was sure of it. How could someone be there and vanish so quickly? The idea of ghosts only amused him for a second. Tyler had never believed in such nonsense. No, it had to be a real flesh and blood person. Monsters weren't real, not like in books. People were the true monsters.

Latching the outside door, Tyler decided there was nothing of use in the garage. In reality, he was too terrified to stay in the garage after his encounter. He tried to open the door which led back into the house but it was locked. It made no sense. How could it have been locked? Then a terrifying thought crept into his mind. The cloaked man may have gone inside, which would account for his absence. He wasn't thoroughly convinced, as he would have heard the door open, but it was the best theory he had.

Knocking on the door, he called for Samantha to let him in but there was no response. Now he was worried. Had the cloaked man found a way in and hurt Samantha? He couldn't wait. If he had to, he would smash a window. Running outside, he looked for another way in.

Looking through the kitchen, Samantha had grabbed a kitchen knife. If someone was out there, she would be ready to defend herself if need be. She had never stabbed a person but assumed it would be easy. It seemed as simple as taking the sharp end and ramming it forward. *I can do that,* she thought.

When the sound of Tyler rummaging around in the garage had stopped, she got worried. She wanted to check on him but thought better of it. He was most likely searching at the far end of the garage and she just couldn't hear him anymore.

Then she heard creaking on the outside deck. Ducking down behind the counter, she inched forward towards the sliding glass door. If the cloaked man was out there, she wanted to get a good look at him. But when she peered around the corner, he was nowhere to be seen.

That was when she remembered the additional door in the house. It had been such a strangely placed door she had forgotten all about it.

For some odd reason, the person who built the house had added an additional door to the bathroom. It led to the outside screened in porch. It, of course, locked with a deadbolt and at the knob. Unfortunately, she had not locked it. For all she knew, the cloaked man was making his way inside while she sat there.

With lightning speed, she raced towards the bathroom and stepped inside without a second thought. She nearly had a heart attack when she saw the man standing there, the door wide open. He reached out to her and she instinctively slashed at him with the knife. The metal clipped his arm, just below the shoulder. He jumped back in pain, a small trickle of blood leaking over his jacket. When Samantha lunged at him again, he turned around and ran back out the door. Without a moment's hesitation, she slammed the door shut and locked it.

Heavy footfalls ran across the deck and crunched back into the dirt. When she could no longer hear them, she picked herself up off the bathroom floor and headed back towards the garage. Tyler should have been back in by now. Worried, she tried to turn the handle. It didn't budge. Looking down at it, she realized it was locked.

"What in the hell?" She asked as she unlocked the door. How had it ended up locked? She hadn't touched the door after Tyler went into the garage. Tyler must have locked it on his way out. It was the only explanation. But why would he do that? She shrugged and twisted the knob yet again. This time it turned and the door swung open.

To her surprise, Tyler was nowhere to be found. The door leading outside was wide open and swaying in the breeze. For some unknown reason, Tyler had locked the garage door and went out the back. None of it made any sense. Not wanting to come face to face with the cloaked man, she shut and locked the outside door and headed back inside. She felt awful thinking only of herself and her safety but did it all the same.

Tyler would have to fend for himself. After what he had done to her, she didn't care.

But is it worth his life? She asked herself. Was it fair to leave him outside with the cloaked man with no help because he had slept with her sister? She did not know. But she was safe for now, and that's all she cared about. Running off into the woods after Tyler would be no help to anyone. There was no way of knowing where he had gone. It would be foolish.

Feeling better about her decision, she raced into her room and grabbed her cell phone. Praying there would be some sort of signal, she tried to dial the police. The call would not go through. "Shit," She said as she gripped the knife tighter. There was truly no way out of this hell.

A knocking came at the front door. "Tyler?" She called out. When there was no response, she started to cry. The cloaked man was back. It sounded as if he were punching the door with his fist. Soon, it changed to a heavy thud of his foot. Wildly, the man kicked the door while Samantha cried inside. Then something heavy slammed against the door nearly splintering it. It sounded like a hammer. It banged again and then clattered to the ground. All of sudden, it all stopped and the cloaked man was gone.

She didn't dare look outside for fear the man would be standing there waiting. Instead, she made sure the curtains were closed and she sat in the corner of the room. Praying to God that he would keep Tyler safe. She hated being alone in the cabin now. "Please let my family get home already," she pleaded. The clock on the far side of the room read twelve-forty-five. They should be back in a few hours and they could finally get the hell out of this place. All she had to do was wait it out.

After leaving the garage, Tyler had decided to make his way towards the sliding glass door. He hoped Samantha would let him in. That was when he saw the cloaked man walking away from the house. He vanished into the tree line. With the hammer gripped tightly in his hands, he decided he was going to go after him. There was no way he was going to let this torment continue.

As quickly and quietly as he could manage, Tyler followed after the man into the woods. The cloaked man walked casually through the trees. Tyler was only a few yards behind him. Readying his hammer, he prepared to sprint and take him down.

Right then, the cloaked man turned around a large tree, breaking the line of sight. Worried he would get away, Tyler bolted towards the tree. As he whipped around it, he brought the hammer up over his head, ready to strike. What he saw then he could not explain. Nothing. Somehow the man was gone.

It didn't make any sense. He had only lost sight of him for a few seconds. How could he have lost him? Tyler couldn't believe it. He started to wonder if they weren't dealing with a man at all. Maybe it *was* some sort of spirit or magical creature in the woods. Knowing the idea was preposterous, he checked the ground for any sign of movement.

There was nothing there. It was as if the man didn't exist at all. But Tyler had seen him, clear as day. Somehow the hooded figured could vanish. Tyler walked deeper into the woods, looking for any sign of the cloaked man. If he were real, there had to be something. A person didn't just vanish.

The sounds of the running river were a distant moan in his ears. He was worried he had traveled too far. It had been at least fifteen minutes and still, he had found no sign of the man. He had to give up. He had to get back to Samantha. She was all alone in the house. He spun on his heel and headed back towards the cabin.

Silence only made the situation worse. It had been twenty minutes and the man had not come back. Tyler was still gone. The worst thoughts ran through her head and she did her best to quiet them down. It was no use. The image of Tyler beaten to death with a hammer flooded through her mind and she cried on the kitchen floor.

It couldn't end that way. She was furious with him for sleeping with her sister. Last night, after hearing the faint moans of sexual desire from behind closed doors, she had wished death upon the both of them. Now, she felt like an utter fool. Had her wish come true? She had only thought it out of anger. In no way did she mean it.

Maybe this thing terrorizing them was not human. She wondered if it were some sort of avenging spirit that was there because of her. Samantha had never openly believed in ghosts, not wanting to get laughed at by her friends and family. But she always marveled in the wonder that they could exist. Now, she was almost certain they did. They had to. But a spirit would have no trouble getting in the house.

She looked down at the kitchen knife still shaking in her hands. She noticed the small stain of blood from where she had cut the man's arm. "They sure as hell don't bleed either," she said aloud. It was true. No matter what lore you believed in, ghosts didn't bleed. It had to be a real person. It had to be some psycho living in the woods, hunting people for fun. The thought somehow terrified her even more than ghosts.

Something clattered in the garage and she froze in horror. The man was back and he was in the garage. Staring at the door which led to it, she shivered in fear. The doorknob moved back and forth as if someone was testing it. Thankfully, it was locked.

The knob stopped turning and was followed by a sound of destruction from inside the garage. Shelves were toppled to the ground. Tools were thrown against the garage door. Glass was broken. It went on for five minutes before stopping abruptly.

Samantha did not move for a whole minute. She sat there staring at the door, expecting the knob to start turning. She screamed when someone knocked on the sliding glass door to her left. She curled on the floor, hidden by the cabinets, and cried. That was when Tyler's voice broke the silence.

"Samantha, please let me in. I think that guy is back. Please hurry."

She bolted upright and craned her neck to see Tyler standing at the glass door. Quickly, she jumped up and unlocked the door. Tyler slid it open as if his life depended on it. Once he was inside, Samantha slammed it shut and locked it again. Looking out around the property, she saw no sign of the cloaked man.

Turning back around, she threw her arms around Tyler.

"I'm so glad to see you," she said. "He was here. He was in *there.*" She pointed to the garage.

"It's ok. I'm here now. We're going to get out of this. I promise."

They curled up together on the kitchen floor and stayed like that for a long time. Neither wanted to move. Samantha could hear his heart beating and it seemed to calm her down. She took solace in the fact that her family would be back to the cabin soon and they could leave. She wished the cloaked man would go away and things would go back to normal. Unfortunately for Samantha, her wish would not come true.

XI Written in Blood

Following the river, Ashley made her way back towards the cabin. She had been walking for a couple hours and knew it couldn't be much further. She wanted to see Tyler again. Maybe she could talk him into a round two. He had been an amazing lover. She just hoped he didn't make it into more than it was. It was just meaningless sex for her. She felt empty since her boyfriend left her and she needed a release. Sure, she felt bad doing that to her sister, but she couldn't help it. Tyler was amazing.

After the vacation was over, they would cut off the affair and Samantha would be none the wiser. It was nothing more than a temporary fling. But she couldn't help but lust for it. Samantha had chosen well for herself. She had quite the man. Ashley realized she was actually jealous of her sister. It seemed Ashley only ever came across men interested in sex and left the next morning. If they did stay long enough to form a relationship, they quickly turned dysfunctional. Deep down it angered her. Still, she did not want to take Tyler from her.

With the river as her guide, Ashley continued to walk. The hours seemed to stretch on for days. The only thing to keep her company was the sound of running water and the cicadas in the trees. Occasionally, a bird would make its presence known high above her. The great outdoors had never been a passion of her and most of its beauty went over her head.

What looked like a piece of orange plastic caught her eye across the river. It was obscured by thick brush, making it impossible to discern what it was. It could have been Wesley's kayak. If so, he might be nearby and need help.

“Wesley,” she called out and her voice echoed through the trees. Somewhere in the distance, a hawk cawed in response. When she heard nothing else, she decided to cross the river. Being relatively calm, she figured it would be easy. She slipped off her shoes and stepped one foot into the water.

“Oh my god, that’s cold.” She said. Her foot slid on a slick rock beneath the surface and she nearly tumbled in. “Shit.”

Gaining her balance, she gently slipped her other foot beneath the water and slowly trekked across. She slipped a couple times but never once fell in. Finally, she made it across. Her bare feet sunk into the mud on the bank and she fell to her knees, covering her khaki shorts. “You’ve gotta be kidding me,” she said as she pulled herself to her feet.

Now, she stared directly at the small bit of orange in the bush. Barely an inch stuck out from the greenery. It was a miracle she had been able to see it at all. Grabbing it with both hands, she pulled the object free. It slid from the bush and crashed into the mud. Ashley stared down at Wesley’s kayak. He had to be nearby, she was sure of it. “Wesley,” she cried again. Still, no answer.

“He must have headed back towards the cabin,” she thought aloud. It made perfect sense. He had washed ashore and got his bearings. After that, he headed back towards the cabin. For all she knew, he was sitting on the porch with Samantha and Tyler at that very moment, waiting for the rest of the family to make it back.

The thought renewed her spirit and she began to head off down the river, not crossing back over. In a hurry, she stumbled across the bank sinking in the mud as she went. After another hour of walking, she came to a point in the river she recognized. It wouldn’t be much longer now and she knew it.

Bending left, the river ran past a small shed and she realized it was the shed which belonged to the cabin. She had finally made it back! Before she could cross, however, she noticed movement on the other side of the river heading away from the home. Walking silently around the trees was Tyler. She couldn't believe her luck. Maybe he was out taking a walk to clear his head. She could meet up with him, have a quickie in the trees, and head back inside. Everything would be great.

Before she could call out to him, she noticed something strange in his hand. Sunlight glinted off the stainless-steel blade of a kitchen knife. It was incredibly odd. Ashley tried to think of one logical reason he would be carrying one through the woods but couldn't.

After a moment, she decided she didn't care. Instead, she would sneak across the river and catch up with him. Taking him by surprise, she would have her way with him. It would be exciting and wonderful. Ashley couldn't wait. Stepping into the water again, she made her way quickly across the calm river.

Once on the other side, she struggled to find Tyler again. He seemed to vanish into thin air. Ashley thought about calling out to him but thought better of it. She wanted to surprise him. Dead leaves crunched on the ground in the distance and she decided to head towards it.

After about ten minutes of searching, she caught a glimpse of movement up ahead. It was impossible to tell if it were Tyler or not. The trees had become far too dense. Peering around a tree, she saw nothing. Suddenly, there was a sharp pain in the middle of her back and she let out a muffled scream. A gloved hand had pressed up against her mouth and held it shut. The pain came back four more times before she realized the horrible truth. Someone was stabbing her.

The last strike struck her spine and she felt her legs give way. The pain was excruciating and Ashley tried desperately to scream but the attacker kept her mouth firmly covered. White hot pain erupted in her side and she realized the stabbing had started up again. Tears rolled down her cheeks and she did her best to flail her arms to escape.

A bitter coldness sank into her body unlike any she had ever felt before. A stream of urine seeped down her leg. Darkness crept into her vision and she slowly began to lose consciousness. Then she felt the cold steel against her throat. "Please." She mumbled under the hand of her attacker but it did not matter. The knife was yanked across her throat, spilling her blood against the tree in front of her. Within seconds, her body was limp and lifeless.

The scene was a gruesome one, though there were no people around to see it. Ashley's body had been propped against a tree with a kitchen knife protruding from her forehead. Her eyes were frozen open in a look of utter fear. A small stream of blood trickled down her face. Under the body, a crimson lake had gathered and mixed with her urine. On the tree above the mutilated body was a message written in Ashley's blood. *Whore.*

XII Please Don't Go

Outside the cabin, things had remained quiet for some time. Samantha and Tyler still curled up on the kitchen floor. They were beginning to think the attacker had finally left them alone. Tyler pulled away from his wife and checked the sliding glass door. There was no sign of him anywhere. The tree line was clear and the clearing was empty. Nothing. It seemed they were safe for the moment.

"We need to check the house, make sure everything is locked," Tyler said. "We can't risk him getting in here."

"What about my family? They've got to be on their way back by now. They're going to run into him."

"We can't think about that right now. If we don't keep ourselves safe, there will be no one to help your family later."

Samantha nodded and stood up from the kitchen floor. Brushing off the bit of dirt on her arm, she stared at Tyler waiting for instructions. He looked at her and thought for a moment. "Alright," he said finally. "We're going to go room by room and check every window and every door. We need to make sure everything is latched and locked."

Samantha nodded and followed behind Tyler as they went to each room. First, they checked the master bedroom where Samantha's parents had slept. It shared a hallway with the garage door and had its own sliding glass door which led to the backyard. It was the one room they had not stepped foot in yet. Relieved to see the door was shut and locked, they checked all the windows. They too were locked.

Heading back into the hall, they double checked the garage door, sliding glass door, and all the windows in the living room. Everything was fine. It wasn't until they made their way into their bedroom that they found anything suspicious. One window in their bedroom had been left unlatched. Ashley quickly locked it and looked over at Tyler. He shook his head. There was no way anyone had come in. They would have heard the window open.

Next, they headed into Ashley's room and checked the windows. Samantha stared at the bed with disgust, knowing what had happened the night before with her sister. The bed sheets were thrown wildly across the bed and Samantha could see a stain on the black sheet. Bile rose in her throat and she left the room. Tyler checked the windows and looked back at the bed. He stared at it for a few seconds and then walked out of the room.

The remainder of the house was secure. Satisfied every window and every door had been locked, the couple made their way to the living room and sat on the couch. Samantha had to resist the urge to cuddle up against her husband. Though she was scared, she couldn't bring herself to rely on him. Seeing the bed, that stain, put things into perspective for her. It made it real. When they made it back home she would be filing for divorce.

"Should we take the car and head into town for help?" Samantha asked.

"I still think we should stay here and wait for your family. We will need to warn them."

"What if we left a note?"

"What if they don't read it in time?"

"Well," she needed to choose her words carefully. "Maybe one of us goes."

"Split up? Are you crazy?"

She shook her head.

"No, we need to stick together."

"Tyler, the danger is only here at the cabin. If one of us were to leave, it would reduce the risk of being harmed. One of us would be out of danger."

"And I suppose you think it should be you who leaves?"

"You're God damned right I do. I'm not staying in this place alone."

"What the hell makes you think I want to?"

"Tyler, I don't really care what you want. You fucked my sister, remember? I can show you the stain on the bed as a reminder. God, you're an unbelievable prick."

"It was a mistake, Samantha. You have to believe I didn't plan it. Your sister came on to me."

"Yeah, and you came inside of her. It doesn't matter who started it. You sure as *fuck* finished it."

Samantha had screamed the last words and jumped up from the couch. "I don't give a shit what you say. If you really cared about me, you would want me out of here. You would want me out of danger. I'm taking the keys and getting in the car. I'll drive into town and bring the police back. You stay here, keep the doors locked, and watch for my family. If we just sit here on our thumbs, we'll most likely die."

Tyler sat in silence, staring at his wife with seemingly no emotion. No anger, no sorrow, nothing. It seemed like he was trying to process it all.

"Please don't go," he finally said. "I need you here. I can't do this without you."

"Get used to it, asshole. When we get home you're going to be doing a lot by yourself."

He asked what she meant by that but she remained silent. Instead, she stormed to the bedroom, grabbed the keys, and pushed her way towards the door. Tyler tried to stop her but she brushed past him. In a last-ditch effort, he tried to push the door shut but she flung it open and ran outside. She jumped inside the Jeep and locked the door.

"Please don't do this," he cried. "He could still be out there. I can't keep you safe if you leave. Please don't go."

"I have to. Stay here and wait for my family," she said through the window, her voice coming across muffled. With that, she slammed the

Jeep in reverse and backed down the driveway. She cried as she turned on to the main road and headed off down the street. Leaving him there was the hardest thing she had ever done. All kinds of terrible thoughts rose to her mind. What if the attacker returned and killed him? But it didn't matter. If she had stayed and the attacker returned, he would kill her too. Then there would be no one to save her family. She had to get help. She had to try.

Tyler cried in the driveway as he listened to the engine in the distance. It grew softer and softer and he realized she was not coming back. He didn't blame her. He had messed up and badly. *What the hell was I thinking?* He thought. Their relationship was over, he knew it. A terrible feeling in the pit of his stomach rose and knotted like some sort of sickening roller coaster ride. It was all his fault. Ashley had been a mistake and now there was no taking it back. He would lose the best thing that had ever happened to him.

Wiping tears from his eyes, he stared at Helen and Dan's SUV. Immediately, the tears stopped flowing and his blood ran cold. In the attempt to stop Samantha from leaving, he had not noticed the smashed windshield and slashed tires.

"What the fuck?" He said aloud, almost startling himself. "Why would he only destroy one..." Then a terrible thought occurred to him. What if he wanted them to use the Jeep? What if it was a trap? Samantha could be in danger.

Something reflected off the SUV's paint and caught Tyler's eye. They widened as he saw the man standing behind him. Quickly, he spun around but there was no one there. His heart banged in his chest like a drum solo. His knees almost gave out as he ran back inside the house and shut the door.

"Fuck this," he said, heading to the kitchen. Pulling a kitchen knife from the wooden block, he said, "I'm going to end this right now." With that, he checked the entire house again. When it turned up empty, he headed out the sliding glass door and into the woods, determined to find their attacker if it was the last thing he ever did.

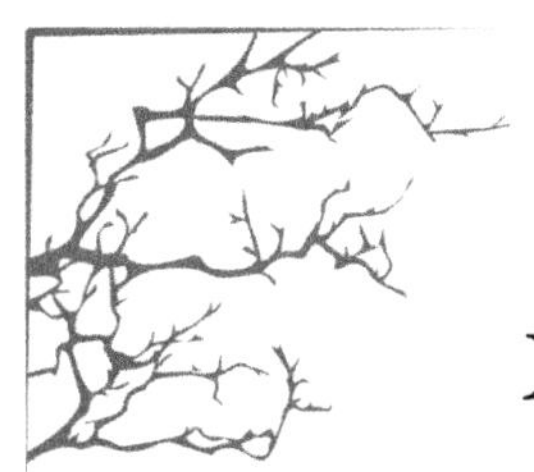

XIII Giving Up

Dan and Helen had checked every which way they could think of by the river. It had been a couple of hours. If Wesley had washed ashore, they would have found him by now. They couldn't keep up the search. If they stayed out much longer, it would be dark before they got back home. They had to head back.

Dan figured they would head back to the cabin where he would take a car into town to call for help. They needed search and rescue out here looking for his son. Something was very wrong. Maybe the current had carried Wesley farther than the rest. There was no way of telling how far.

Helen and Dan met back up at the designated point by the river and Dan told her what he thought. She agreed. She had seen no signs of Wesley either, not even his kayak. She feared the worst and wanted to get a search party out as soon as possible. If Wesley was in trouble, they would get him the help he needed. They weren't about to lose a child on this trip.

"Let's head back," she said giving her husband a hug. With that, the couple turned around and began to follow the river back towards shelter.

XIV Into the Woods

He walked cautiously, hearing the pounding beat of his heart like thunder in his chest. The man was out here somewhere and he knew it. With his wife having left for help, he knew he couldn't just sit on his hands. Deep down he knew she had left for more than just help. She couldn't stand to be around him. After what he had done to her, he no longer blamed her.

Wishing he could take it all back, he gripped the knife tighter. Walking through the woods, he looked all around. Eventually, he would stumble upon him, he had to. Something crunched to his left and he proceeded towards the noise. Tyler held the knife with an outstretched arm. Another noise broke the air only this time it was straight ahead. Carrying on, he thought he saw movement.

Fighting back the urge to run back towards the house, Tyler swallowed hard and headed towards the noise. All around him, the noise seemed to get louder. Branches swaying in the wind, birds chirping loudly, and the roar of the distant river echoed in his ears. Tyler thought he heard a soft whisper on the wind but decided it was only his imagination.

"Tyler," truly hearing a voice whisper, he froze in his tracks. Desperately, he looked around but saw no one. He was alone in the woods. But the voice had been real, he was sure of it.

Refusing to speak, Tyler kept searching. His hands shook uncontrollably. At any moment, he thought he might drop the knife. Whoever was out here was toying with him. Worse, they were hunting him. It was all a game to this lunatic out in the woods. He was enjoying it.

Tyler stepped around a tree and saw a figure in the distance. They were slightly obscured by a nearby tree but he could tell their back was turned. It was the perfect time to strike. He wouldn't hold back. Tyler was going to end this torture once and for all.

Her cell phone still had no signal. She had been driving for nearly fifteen minutes at sixty miles an hour and still had hardly covered any ground. She cursed her cheating husband for coming up with the idea of traveling to the middle of nowhere. There was no help, no city close by, and no cell signal. It was almost as if he had planned...

A cold and utterly terrifying idea crept into her mind like vines growing on the branch of a tree, strangling the bark. It was a thought she could not shake no matter how hard she tried. What if Tyler *had* planned all of this? Did he hire someone to terrorize her or worse? Was he too afraid to leave her for Ashley and instead resorted to having her killed? Maybe it was much worse than all of that. Maybe Tyler had snapped and was trying to kill her himself.

“No, that’s crazy. It couldn’t be-“

She thought about the attacker at the cabin. He never once appeared when Tyler was near. They seemed to exist separately of each other, never daring to be in the same vicinity.

“No way, I can’t seriously think he would do that?” Talking aloud to herself made her feel crazy but provided a sense of calm. Saying her ridiculous thoughts aloud made them sound silly and implausible. But deep down she felt something wasn’t right.

Slamming on the brakes, she came to a stop with dust and dirt swirling up around her like a twister. She had cut the attacker! Samantha had remembered slicing his arm with the knife. If it was Tyler, he would have the same cut across his arm. If he didn’t, he was safe. It made perfect sense.

She had to turn back. Her family could return to the cabin at any moment and walk into a trap. If Tyler was behind it all, they could be in trouble. She would never get to town and back in time. There was no other option. She had to turn back.

Spinning the wheel as far to the left as it would turn, Samantha stepped on the gas. The little car turned around and accelerated back towards the cabin.

Tyler had run towards the figure in the woods. When he had only been feet away, it spun around and stared at him. It didn't move, it didn't run, it just stared at him. The maneuver caught him so off guard that he stopped in his tracks.

Standing there, staring at him, was the attacker he had seen many times that day. He just stood there as if he were one of the trees in the forest. Wind whistled through the trees somewhere in the distance.

"Who the fuck are you?" Tyler demanded. There was no answer. The man merely stood there, hood pulled over his head and black cloth masked his face. They made eye contact and Tyler nearly pissed in his own pants. There was no fear in those eyes, no worry. It was as if all of this had been planned to perfection.

Suddenly, the man lunged forward a few inches. Tyler fell backward and rolled in the leaves, losing the knife. When he climbed to his feet, he was alone. *How in the hell?* It was impossible. The man had vanished into thin air again. Tyler began to wonder if he were going crazy. Maybe the attacker had been a figment of his imagination.

But that couldn't be. Samantha had seen him too. A supernatural explanation seemed to be the only logical one, though Tyler was still unsure he believed it. However, it seemed this being was able to appear and disappear at a moment's notice.

He had heard ghost stories like it before but never gave them any thought. There wasn't proof of ghosts, none that he had ever seen. It was something paranoid, superstitious people used to explain events they didn't fully comprehend. Now, he wasn't so sure.

Scanning the woods around him, Tyler began to realize he was lost. He had wandered for an indeterminate amount of time and had paid little attention to where he had been going. There was no way of knowing how to get back. If he had been in the right frame of mind, he would have left himself a trail.

He started off in a random direction. The sun was getting low in the sky and fear took hold of him. Tyler started to run. Dodging tree after tree, he finally came to a stop and caught his breath. Bent over with his hands on his knees, he took in deep breaths. Something below him made his heart skip a beat. A pool of red liquid lapped at his shoes, staining them. "What the fu-" He stood up and stared at the mangled mess against the tree. Suddenly, his world went dark.

Samantha raced the sun as she sped down the road towards the cabin. Her family had to be back by now. She couldn't leave them alone with Tyler. He had to be sick. Something had to be wrong. Tyler was not a killer but he had never been a cheater either. Something in his head must have broken down. He slept with her sister and was now out to kill her and possibly her family. She was convinced it was the truth.

If Tyler didn't have a cut on his arm everything would be fine. She and Tyler and the rest of her family could load up in the car and get the hell out. They would never come back to this miserable patch of land out in the middle of nowhere, Florida. But something told her it wasn't meant to be. Something told her nothing would end like she hoped.

She was getting close to the cabin now, she could feel it. The sun was sinking lower in the sky, threatening to cast the world into darkness. Samantha had to make it back before then. She felt like a fool for leaving in the first place. If she was being honest with herself, she had been scared. Terror and disgust with her husband had become too much to bear. Now, she would go back and confront it all head on.

Something stepped out of the trees on the left side of the road and jumped in front of her car. There was no time to steer clear and she plowed into it head on. Skidding to the left, Samantha's car slammed directly into a tree. Her head bounced off the airbag and hit the headrest behind her. The force was enough to knock her out cold.

She did not see the deer roll off the roof of the car and limp into the distance, nursing its wounds. She didn't see the sun slip behind the horizon and cast the world in the afterglow of evening. Samantha did not see any of this while she lay unconscious in her car. But watching from the tree line, the hooded man saw it all.

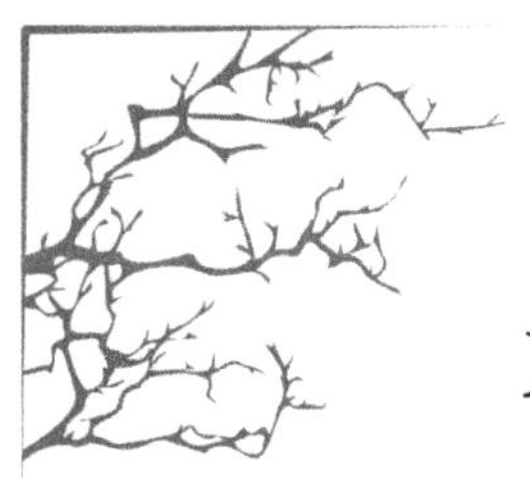

XV The Return

Stumbling back to the cabin, Tyler cried and held back vomit in his throat. What he had seen in the woods had been terrible, grotesque. Pinned against the tree, he had found the body of Samantha's sister, Ashley. There were multiple stab wounds in her back and side, blood drenching her once beige shorts. A look of complete terror had been plastered on her face and a knife, like the one he had been carrying, stuck in her head. The most terrible thing of all had been the word *whore* written in her blood across the tree.

Whoever had killed her had known about their affair. Did it mean he was next? Why would the attacker care? Unless it was Samantha. That had to be it. Then Tyler realized he had seen the attacker in the clearing while standing next to her, but she hadn't seen him. Why hadn't she seen him then? Was she lying? Did she know about the attacker? His list of questions had grown making his head spin, not helping his nausea.

Poor Ashley, he thought, thinking back to the previous night. She had been very much alive only the night before. It seemed impossible for her to be gone. In the blink of an eye, her existence had been extinguished by a madman.

Why didn't he kill me? He thought. Instead, the hooded man had stood there, staring at him. In fact, the hooded man had several chances to kill him and he'd never once taken it. Why? The thought scared Tyler more than anything. Was this murderer merely toying with him? Maybe he wanted to break him down and punish him for sleeping with Ashley. All kinds of horrifying thoughts raced through his mind at the speed of light. He was almost certain he would black out again.

Looking down at his hands, he realized they were stained with blood. “Oh my God,” he cried as he ran over to the sink. For ten minutes, he scrubbed at his hands, ruining two hand towels in the process. Burying the towels deep in the trash can, he sat on the couch and cried.

“What the fuck is going on?” He sobbed into his hands, feeling pathetic. None of it made sense. There had been plenty of opportunities for the hooded man to kill Tyler. Why had he been spared but Ashley killed? The knife sticking out of her skull had been the same one he dropped in the woods, at least he thought it was. There was blood on his hands, though he didn't remember touching the body. Something was wrong. A throbbing pain sprang up on his left arm just below the shoulder, but he ignored it. There was too much to process.

For what seemed like an hour, Tyler sat on the couch in his misery. “What am I going to tell Samantha?” He thought about it. “What am I going to tell Helen and Dan if they come back?” He decided he would keep quiet. It would do them no good knowing Ashley's fate before help arrived. In fact, it might make them irrational.

The sun had long since fallen behind the horizon and darkness engulfed the cabin. Tyler realized this and jumped up to turn on all the lights, feeling vulnerable. He curled up on the couch and prayed Samantha would return soon with the police.

“Finally,” a voice cried out in the distance. Tyler perked up on the couch and recognized it as Dan. They had made it back from their trip. His heart began to race again. He would have to tell them about the man in the woods, how Samantha had left to get help. They would have questions but he would have no answers.

Frantically, he tried to rehearse what he would tell them. Before he had time, however, they stepped up to the sliding glass door and tapped on the glass. “Tyler,” Dan yelled. He didn't have to say anything more. Tyler walked and flipped the metal latch-up and slid the door open.

Once they were inside, he shut the door and locked it with lightning speed. Dan and Helen did not seem to notice. "My God, have we got a story for you," Dan began. "Where's Samantha and Ashley?"

"Wasn't Ashley with you guys?" He lied, knowing full well where the soon-to-be decomposing body was.

"She was, but she came back on her own. She should have been here by now. Wesley didn't happen to come home too, did he?"

Tyler shook his head.

"Shit." Dan started to pace, clearly upset. Helen tried to calm him down but it was no use. "How can they not be here? And where the hell did Samantha go?" Dan was practically yelling now.

"Dan, I need to tell you something. It's going to sound crazy but it's all true."

Dan looked at him as if he had just been struck. He cocked his head and narrowed his eyes at Tyler.

"Samantha took the car to go for help. She headed into town."

"Help? Help for what?"

Tyler told him everything, leaving out the affair. He hoped Samantha would never mention it to them either, no matter what. When the family finally learned she was dead they would not need to know she had destroyed Tyler and Samantha's marriage as well. Some things were better left unsaid. Instead, Tyler talked all about the man in the woods, how he had been stalking and terrorizing them.

"That's when we fought about splitting up or staying together. I insisted we both stay here, wait for you guys, and all leave together. But she thought it would be best if she went for help while she still could."

"You're joking with me, right?" Dan demanded. "You have to be trying to prank us, that's what this is. Samantha, Ashley, Wesley come on out. It's really not funny."

Tyler gripped Dan by the shoulders and gave him a quick shake.

"Dan, it's not a joke. I wish it were. Someone is out there and they will probably be back. We have to get the fuck out of here."

"If what you're saying is true," Helen broke in. "That means Ashley and Wesley are out there with this madman. We have to find them. We can't just leave them out there."

"What happened to you guys?" Tyler asked. "How did you get split up?"

Dan explained the bend in the river and how the path on the map had taken them to the rapids. He went on to explain how they were capsized and separated from Wesley. When Dan finished talking he looked at Tyler as if waiting for an explanation but Tyler only stood there in astonishment.

"That's not possible," he said. "I drew those maps myself. I went over them multiple times. There's no way they were wrong."

"Well, they were, Tyler. You almost got us killed. And what's worse, my kids are out there with a psychotic *asshole.* We need to find them."

"I'm so sorry. I don't know what happened. But we can't go out there looking for them, not in this darkness. We'd never have a chance. The best thing to do is to sit here and wait for Samantha to return with the police."

Dan shook his head and headed towards the sliding glass door. Grabbing the flashlight off the kitchen counter he said, "I can't just wait around. I have to find them."

Before he could open the door, Helen pushed her way in front of him.

"I don't like it either, but Tyler's right. It's too dark out there. We'd only get lost too. The best thing we can do is wait for the police. When they get here we can have search and rescue comb these woods for our kids. Everything will be fine. Tyler said the person never really hurt them. Maybe he's just some hillbilly in the woods who likes to scare people for fun."

Tyler thought of Ashley's mutilated body and shuddered.

"Please don't go out there." She begged.

There was a look in his eye that said he understood the logic of their argument but he just didn't care. It was obvious to Tyler he was going to go anyway. There was only one thing he could do, but he didn't want to. He couldn't let Dan go out there and find his daughter the way she was. It would destroy him.

"Wait," Tyler said, grabbing the flashlight from Dan. "I'll go. I've been out there a couple of times today. I think I might be able to navigate back here. Besides, it's my fault you guys got separated in the first place. I think it's best if I do this."

"Oh God, Tyler. Are you sure?" Helen asked.

"Honestly, no. But I'm going to anyway."

Dan extended his arm and proffered his hand. Tyler looked down and shook it with confidence.

"You're a good man, Tyler." He said. "I can come with you if you-"

"No." Tyler snapped. "I mean, stay here and look after Helen. If that guy comes back, at least you will have each other."

Dan nodded and Tyler headed out the door. Once again, he found himself in the terrible silence that was the woods. Now, it was far more menacing. His entire body shook as he made his way across the moonlit clearing and into the trees. It had become a familiar feeling for him and yet it still scared him half to death. Every sound made his skin crawl. He thought he could feel the burn of something watching him from afar. He resisted the urge to run back towards the house and lock himself inside.

After a few yards, he heard something creak through the woods. At first, he thought it was the wind in a tree, but then he heard it again. Now he knew it was footsteps. They were light, almost masked by the wind. It was difficult to see in the utter darkness. The moon was obscured by the tops of the giant trees and only a trickle of pale light made it to the forest floor. There was a crack behind him and he froze in terror. He knew he would see the cloaked man if he turned around. Holding his flashlight like a baton, he slowly spun on his heel, ready to face his attacker.

Falling from the driver side door, Samantha landed on the ground with a loud *thump.* Her back hurt and her head ached but she was alive.

Shaking off her nerves, she started to walk down the road. It was pitch black and she was terrified, knowing the hooded man could be out there watching her. But there was no other option. The car was totaled. The house could not be far away. She assumed it would take less than thirty minutes to walk to it.

With her feet shuffling on the dirt road, she headed forward. Dust kicked up around her feet, creating a thin layer of dirt around her ankles. With a slight limp, possibly from a sprained ankle, she carried forward.

Samantha's head throbbed like someone had bashed in her skull with a baseball bat. She wanted the pain to subside and for her head to clear. Thoughts of concussion crossed her mind but she did her best to shake it off. After all, nothing could be done about it now.

Wind barreled through the trees around her but she did not hear it. The blood rushing through her veins was too loud. She tried to focus on something else but found it hard. Behind her, a small plume of white smoke rose from the car's engine. If she had seen it, she would have been worried about starting a forest fire. But she carried on, oblivious to the danger behind her, knowingly heading towards the one ahead of her.

Battered and bruised, Wesley fell into the clearing and nearly kissed the dirt. Dark patches of mud and dirt caked his face and hands. Minor scratches and scrapes littered his body from the tumble into the rapids. His hair was matted with a mixture of sweat and river water.

With as much speed as he could muster, he ran towards the house and flung himself on the back porch. No energy left, he began to crawl. With a filthy hand, he smacked against the sliding glass door, leaving a ring of filth behind.

Helen was first to respond and ran to the door with tears in her eyes. Flinging it open, she dragged her exhausted son inside. "What happened to you?" She asked as Dan closed the door and helped drag Wesley to the couch.

"Water," he asked and waited for his father to pour him a glass.

He drank it down in one gulp and sighed.

"We have to get out of here now." His hoarse voice cracked.

"As soon as Samantha comes back with the police and if Tyler can find Ashley, we're leaving," Dan said.

"No, no. We can't. We have to leave now. It isn't safe."

"I don't care how unsafe it is. We're not leaving without your sisters and Tyler."

"Dad, you don't get it. It's Tyler!"

Dan looked at him for a moment, cocking his head to the left. Scratching his temple, he said, "What are you talking about, son? What about Tyler?"

"Tyler is trying to kill us."

Dan laughed at this.

"You must have hit your head on a rock, boy. Tyler is out there, risking his life to find your sister. He's not trying to kill-"

"Dad," Wesley said with a somber tone. "He isn't *trying* to kill. He already *has.*"

Dan took a step back and stared at his son in awe. Wesley could tell he was struggling to process it all. There was no easy way to tell him.

"Dad, Ashley is dead. I found her body in the woods. It was Tyler. *He* fucking killed my sister!"

Dan fell to his knees, staring at his son. Helen placed her hand over her mouth and held back tears. The family was being torn to shreds in a matter of seconds. Dan shook his head and stared at the floor.

"No, I don't believe it," He said. "You must have been seeing things. There's no way-"

"I wasn't seeing things, Dad. Jesus, *fuck,* it was her. The sick bastard cut her throat."

Tears started to stream down Wesley's face. He attempted to wipe them away but changed his mind. Instead, he let them run free. Placing his face in his hands, he cried. Helen knelt next to Wesley and wrapped her arms tight around him. The two of them cried as they embraced. Dan still sat on the floor and shook his head.

"How do you know it was Tyler?" Dan asked.

Tyler told the story to the best of his ability. First, he said he had gone into the rapids and was scraped against the rocks for what seemed like miles. Eventually, he was thrown against the river bank. Crawling free of the mud, he lay under the trees for an amount of time he could not determine. Finally, he pulled himself to his feet and started to walk.

At first, he was dizzy and walked in the wrong direction, continuing downstream. After a while, he realized his mistake and turned around. The rest of the day he walked back up river. After night had fallen, he found where the river banked left and knew it was where the cabin sat. Carefully, he made his way across.

He found himself temporarily turned around in a patch of woods. He walked for an hour before stumbling across Ashley's body. He spared his parents the gruesome details. It was then he had found Tyler. He had been standing nearby, watching him. He noted something very strange. It seemed like he had been talking to someone.

"I think he might be sick," Wesley said. "Like schizophrenic or whatever. He might have no idea he's even doing it. But, regardless, I ran. He started to chase me and eventually caught me. We fought, I think I broke his nose. After that, I rammed the back of his head against a tree. Pretty sure he went out cold. I ran forever before falling into the clearing and finding the cabin."

Helen had pulled away from her son and stood next to Dan, who was still crouched on the floor. The pair of them cried as he told his story. Clearly, it confirmed it had not been a hallucination or a sick prank.

"Why would he do this?" Dan asked again.

"I told you, I think something's wrong with him. He changed the maps on us and killed Ashley. Now he's trying to kill us." Then he stopped, remembering something. "Wait, did you say Samantha was getting the police?"

Dan nodded and Helen said, "Yes, while we were gone, they were being terrorized by a man. She took the car to town to get help. Do you think it was Tyler the whole time or does he have a friend out there? Wait, why would he let her leave?"

"Who knows. We won't know until we catch him or Samantha comes back. *If* she comes back."

Double vision clouded his eyes and pain pulsed in his skull. Tyler stumbled through the woods and into the clearing. A small trickle of blood dripped from his nose and landed on his pants, though he did not notice.

Up ahead, he could see the cabin. Light emanated from inside like a lighthouse on the ocean. He could see Dan and Helen inside, except there was someone else now. After a few minutes of staring, he realized it was Wesley. He was relieved to see the rest of Samantha's family had made it out of the woods alive. For some reason, Ashley was the only person the attacker had killed.

He began to wonder if the person terrorizing them was an ex-boyfriend of Ashley's or someone she had wronged in the past. It seemed the attacker was only out to get her. But deep down he knew that couldn't be true.

Deciding he didn't care at the moment, Tyler headed towards the cabin as quickly as he could. As soon as he approached the sliding glass door, he pulled it open. Helen began to scream and Dan tackled him in a second. Confused, Tyler tried to struggle but found himself overpowered. Now, in a headlock, Dan asked him questions he didn't understand.

"What are you talking about?"

"Why are you doing this? Why did you kill Ashley?"

"I didn't kill anyone. I found her out there like that. I couldn't bring myself to tell you until after the police got here."

"Sure, the police. Or did you kill Samantha and hide her body. She never left to get the police, did she?"

"Yes, she did!"

Wesley helped Dan lift Tyler into a chair and held him down. Dan barked at Helen to find something to secure him with. Finding a roll of duct tape in one of the drawers, she handed it off. Using up the whole roll, Wesley and Dan taped him to the chair.

"Please, what are you doing?" Tyler cried. "I didn't kill anyone. I don't know what you're-"

"Save your shit, Tyler. Wesley told me everything. He's the one who gave you that bloody nose."

"You!" Tyler cried. "It was you!"

"Yes, it was me. You fucking attacked me, remember?"

"That's not what happened at all. Dan, you have to believe me. I was jumped from behind out there. Someone hit me in the face and knocked me out. I never even saw who did it."

"And you expect me to believe you over my own son? Especially after you sabotaged the kayak trip?"

"I didn't sabotage anything. I checked those maps over and over."

"You led us directly into the rapids on purpose. You hoped they would kill us."

"No, I didn't. It's not poss-"

"But it is possible. It happened. We followed your map and almost died."

Tyler had been sure he had studied that map well. There was no chance he had made a mistake. The route he had highlighted should have been safe. There was no question about it. They must have gone the wrong way by mistake, though he wasn't about to tell them that. They were angry enough.

Wesley left the room as Dan continued to interrogate Tyler. When he came back, the color had run out of his cheeks. "Dad," he said in almost a whisper. "Look what I found in his bag." He handed a piece of paper that looked like a map. Tyler struggled to see what it was but thought he already knew.

"Explain this, then." Dan held the map in front of Tyler's face. A red line followed the river and went right, unlike the map Dan had been following on the river. "You switched them, didn't you?"

"No! Of course not. That makes no sense. Why would I make two maps and switch them? Why not just make one wrong one and give it to you?"

"Because there's something wrong with you," Dan screamed. "You tried to kill us on the river and when that didn't work, you cut up my daughter. And you probably killed Samantha too. Wesley was right. You're sick, there's something wrong in your head."

"What are you talking about?"

"I saw you out there, Tyler," Wesley said. "You were talking to yourself. It looked like you were telling someone to leave you alone but there was no one there. Have you been seeing things or people or something."

"No, just the person who has been attacking me and Sam-" He stopped, realizing he would now incriminate himself.

"I don't think you really saw anyone attacking. I think it was all in your mind."

"Bullshit, if that's true how come Samantha saw him too?"

"She's not here to vouch for herself is she?"

"Fuck you, look outside. Our car is gone. If I killed her, why would I hide the car and not just leave? Why would I stay?"

"Cause you want to kill the rest of us too. Tell me, did you ever see this attacker when you and Samantha were together?"

Tyler was about to answer yes but went silent. He realized, Wesley was right. Samantha had never seen the attacker when he was around. It seemed she only saw him when he was away from her. Then there was the time in the woods. The man had just stared at him and spared his life. Was Wesley right? Was he sick? He couldn't help but wonder if there really was something wrong with him. But it couldn't be possible. That kind of thing only happened in the movies. In reality, it was unlikely. At least he hoped.

By saying nothing, he seemed to prove Wesley's point. Dan nodded and headed towards the kitchen. Tyler watched with wide eyes as he grabbed a large knife from the kitchen drawer.

"What are you doing, Dan?" Helen asked. Tyler could hear the fear in her voice.

"This son of a bitch took our daughters away from us. Now, I'm gonna take his life."

"Dan, you can't do that. Please stop."

Someone began to pound on the door. The room fell silent for a moment. Finally, a familiar voice cut through and Dan nearly dropped the knife. "Tyler, let me in," Samantha yelled.

Dan raced to the door and flung it open. "Dad?" She asked as he wrapped his arms around her and dragged her inside.

"Oh sweetheart, we thought you were dead."

"What? Why would you think-"

She stopped, seeing Tyler taped to the chair in the dining room.

"Why?" She said, pointing.

"Honey, this might be hard to hear, but we think Tyler might have killed your sister."

Samantha nearly fell to the floor. Instead, she stared at her father with wide eyes. Tears rolled down her cheeks and she quickly brushed them away.

"Ashley's dead? No, you can't be serious." She looked over at Tyler and he saw a rage in her eyes he had never seen before. "You son of a bitch," she screamed and ran at him. With open palms, she smacked him in the face over and over. "Did you do it?" She yelled as she did.

Tyler yelled for her to stop and said he didn't kill anyone. He told Samantha about finding Ashley's body in the woods but didn't tell anyone. Wesley interrupted and told his story about being attacked in the woods. The family began to argue and fight. Dan and Wesley arguing that Tyler was a killer, Tyler defending himself, and Helen telling everyone to be rational.

"I have a way to tell," Samantha screamed, shutting everyone up. Everyone, including Tyler, looked at her. "Earlier, the man was in the house. I cut his arm with a kitchen knife. If Tyler really is the killer, he'll have a mark here." She pointed to her arm just below the shoulder.

Dan nodded and approached Tyler. Lifting his sleeve, everyone gasped in horror. The slice was exactly where Samantha had said it would be, blood still wet on his arm. Tyler began to cry himself. He could not recall getting the cut. His reality was breaking down around him. Maybe Wesley was right.

"Please," he started to cry. "I have no idea what's going on. I didn't do any of it. I don't know how that cut got there. Maybe there *is* something wrong with me. I don't remember any of that. Please, you have to believe me." He looked Samantha in the eyes. "Please, baby. You have to believe me."

"I don't understand," Wesley interrupted. "Why write *whore* above Ashley. What did *that* mean?"

"I didn't write anything. I didn't do it. Please." He was whimpering now, desperate for the family to believe him.

"I know why, " Samantha said. "Last night, Ashley and Tyler slept together."

Dan's eyes grew furious now. He stared daggers at Tyler and gripped the knife tighter in his hand. Tyler knew he had to talk him down before something terrible happened. He did not want to die here, not like this.

"It's true. I made a mistake last night. Ashley caught me in the hall and led me to her room. I shouldn't have done it. I should have said no.

I was weak. But that doesn't mean I killed her. You have to believe me. I would never do anything like that."

"Tyler, you have the cut on your arm. It's the same cut I gave to the man attacking us. Come to think of it, I never saw you when he was around. Pretty convenient, wouldn't you say?"

"But it couldn't have been me. I don't remember doing any of it. I don't even remember getting this cut. It could be from a tree branch in the woods!"

Wesley looked at the rest of the family and shrugged. "I think I'm right. I think he's got multiple personalities or whatever. We can't trust a thing he says."

Tyler shook his head. "How could that be true? I've never had any symptoms of it before. You can't tell me it came out of nowhere just today?"

"I don't know how it works. Maybe that's exactly what happened."

Again, the family started to argue. Tyler continued to tell the family he wasn't sick, though he wasn't quite sure anymore. Helen pleaded for everyone to take a step back while Wesley screamed that his sister was dead because of Tyler. Dan, however, was being oddly silent. He merely gripped the knife in his hand and stared at the ground.

"Hold on," Samantha screamed. "If he is sick, we need to get him help. It won't change what he did to Ashley and I'm not saying any of us have to forgive him, but we need to get him help. We owe him that at the very least."

The room was silent for a whole minute. Dan still stared at the ground. Tyler realized there were tears in his eyes. He had no idea what was going on. He felt as if he had lost his mind. Maybe what Wesley said was true. After all, he had seen the hooded man in the corner of his eye many times only to turn around and be alone. Maybe he really was a figment of his imagination. Desperately, he tried to think of anything that proved the hooded man was real but couldn't. He decided he would allow the family to check him into a hospital to get the help he needed. Especially if Ashley was dead.

He couldn't believe she was gone. There was no reason in the world for him to kill Ashley. Though he figured the family and a jury wouldn't see it that way. He had made a mistake by sleeping with her and his motive could have been to save his relationship. *Jesus Christ, I really fucked up, didn't I?* He thought, thinking of his affair. It had jump-started something he could never have fathomed. His marriage was most definitely over and his life, as he knew it, would be forever changed. God, he hated himself for giving in to temptation.

"No," Dan said suddenly. "This son of a bitch killed my daughter." Before anyone could stop him, he lunged forward with the knife. In one devastating strike, he plunged the knife deep into Tyler's chest. Tyler gasped in pain and stared at the knife in shock and horror. Samantha screamed for her father to stop, but it was too late.

Cold swept over Tyler's body. A thin line of blood flowed over his lips and fell to his shirt below. "Samantha...for...forgive me." He said as his head fell forward and the light that was his life slowly flickered out.

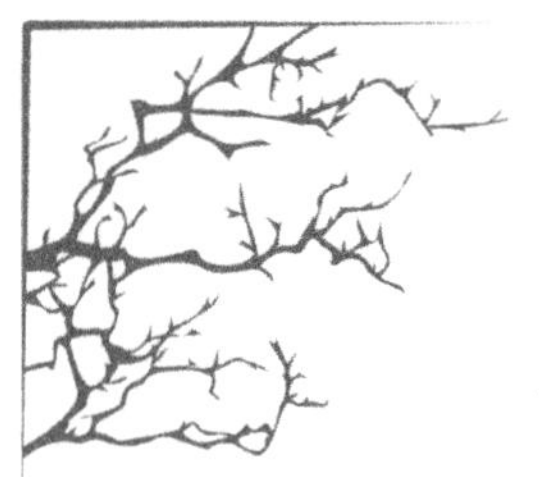

XVI The Body

"**Dan what** in God's name have you done!" Helen screamed.

"Dad, no!"

"Holy fuck," Wesley said.

The family was in utter shock at Dan's actions. He had murdered Tyler in cold blood. There had been no other reason than revenge and anger. With Tyler tied up, there was no threat. They could have gone to the police and had him arrested and committed. There would have been an investigation to prove whether or not he was the killer.

Samantha did not want to admit it, but she had started to doubt Tyler was involved. Something about his reactions had struck her as genuine. She felt as if she knew her husband pretty well. There wasn't a twinkle of dishonesty in his eyes when he spoke. But it didn't matter now. He was dead, never coming back.

"What the *fuck* did you do, dad? You killed him!"

"Can't you see, honey? I had no choice. He killed your sister and tortured you. He would have done it again if we gave him the chance."

"We have no fucking clue if it was him or not. What if you were wrong?"

"What are you talking about? You're the one who pointed out the cut on his arm. It had to be him."

"That doesn't mean kill him!" Her face was red and embers burned in her eyes.

"I did it to protect you, sweetie." He opened his arms and attempted to hug her but she pulled away. At that moment, her father disgusted her. He had ended her husband's life with hardly a second thought.

Even if he had been Ashley's killer, it was a cold and disturbing thing to do.

"No, you did it because you're a coward. You murdered him. You murdered my husband! We should have trusted him. He was part of our family. Instead, we pointed fingers at him when we got scared. Why? Because he made a mistake? I can't..." Bile rose in her throat but she swallowed hard. "Fuck you dad. I hate you. I never want to see you again you god damned murderer."

Before anyone could say anything, Samantha ran to her room and slammed the door. Flinging herself on the bed, she started to sob. The pillow next to her was empty and it only fueled her sorrow. Tyler was gone. There would forever be a hole in her life now.

No, this couldn't be happening. This had to be some sort of lucid nightmare. With tears rolling down her cheeks like rushing waterfalls, she pinched herself on the arm. Again and again, she pinched trying desperately to wake up. Eventually, a bruise formed and she rolled over to Tyler's side of the bed. Snatching up his pillow, she took in a deep breath. It still smelled like his cologne.

Again, the bile rose up in her throat and this time she didn't fight it. Leaning over the side of the bed, she vomited on the hardwood floor. It splashed under the bed, pooling into a disgusting pile of digestion. Wiping her mouth with the back of her hand, she buried her face in Tyler's pillow and cried some more.

This is all my fault, she thought. It was her who had told them about the cut on his arm. For all she knew, it had been a coincidence. He could have been cut by a tree in the woods like he said. It wasn't impossible. A million thoughts began to race through her mind and she thought she would go crazy at any moment. Her head throbbed worse than it had after the car accident.

At some point, her mother had knocked on the door and tried to talk to her but Samantha ignored her. Everything was in shambles. She had lost her husband and her sister in the same day. Now, she would be losing a father too. No matter what happened, she would never talk to him again. Of that she was sure. There could be no room in her life for such a sadistic man.

Samantha eventually fell asleep in her room with Tyler's pillow clutched tightly in her arms. Dan and Wesley were busy wrapping Tyler's body in spare bed sheets they had found in the closet. Opening up the garage door, they placed his body inside.

Dan had wanted to bury the body somewhere in the woods but Wesley said it would be a bad idea. If the police got involved, they would want to know why they had buried the body. A buried body would make Dan look guilty like he tried to cover it up. Dan was completely sure Tyler was the killer. His mind was now at ease knowing he had delivered justice to his baby's killer.

In the morning, he would go out and retrieve his daughter's body and then make the trek into town to notify the police. It would be a long trip, now having no car. But they would deal with that in the morning. Now, Dan decided the best thing they could do is try and get some sleep.

"Sleep? How can we sleep? There could still be a killer on the loose?" Helen said.

"There isn't. He's dead and in the garage. I can assure you of that."

"You can't be sure of that, Dan. You killed our son in law. Do you know what that means?"

"It means you and the rest of our kids are safe from his delusional mind."

"No, it means you've lost a daughter. She's never going to talk to you again and you know it. No matter the outcome. Even if the police investigate and learn he *was* behind it all. She's always going to see you as a killer. Can't you see that?"

Dan shrugged. He didn't believe it. Samantha would eventually come around. After the police found evidence that Tyler had killed

Ashley, she would thank him for what he did. Samantha was a smart girl. She would eventually see the light.

"Wesley, get in your room and lock the door. Try and get some sleep. Helen, let's go to bed. You'll feel better about all of this in the morning. I promise I did what was right for this family. You'll come to see that."

Helen shook her head but followed her husband into the bedroom. The two of them lay motionless on the bed for several hours before finally drifting off to sleep. Dan was ripped from sleep after a nightmare about stabbing Tyler. He could vividly see the blood leaking from his mouth as well as the surprised and terrified look on his face. A cold sweat had broken out on Dan's forehead.

Wiping the sweat away, he rolled onto his side and shut his eyes. These nightmares weren't going to keep him from sleeping. There was nothing he regretted. Keeping his family safe was his job, no matter what. He shut his eyes and fell into a deep sleep, not knowing he would never wake up.

The whole house awoke to a blood-curdling scream from Helen. Wesley made it to the room before Samantha, who was only a few seconds behind him. Helen was plastered against the wall and staring at the bed like she was trying to get as far from it as she could.

Wesley's eyes followed her gaze and spotted his father on the bed, throat cut from ear to ear. Blood covered his chest and stained the bed sheets all around him. Her eyes were shut, telling them he had been killed in his sleep. Maybe it meant he had not suffered. Wesley wasn't sure.

He spun on his heel and stared daggers at Samantha. "Did you fucking do this?"

She looked back at him incredulously.

"You have to be out of your god damned mind." She yelled, wiping a tear from her face. "I would never do something like this."

"He killed your husband and you wanted revenge."

"That's not fucking true and you know it. You and Dad were wrong. The killer is still out there. He fucking killed Tyler for nothing!"

"Bullshit, you cut his throat for killing Tyler. You fucking bitch." He smacked her in the face with all of his force and she toppled to the ground. Helen screamed for them to stop but it was too late. The two of them fought for several moments before Samantha bolted out of the room and into her own.

Before she could shut the door, however, Wesley rammed it with his shoulder, breaking it off one hinge. Grabbing Samantha by the hair, he flung her across the room. Helen entered just in time to see her smash into the nightstand and the contents scattered about the floor.

"Samantha, no. How could you."

A blood-stained knife rested on the floor among the contents of the nightstand. Samantha stared at it like it was radioactive. "You can't seriously believe I put that there."

"What the hell else am I to believe? Who else could have put that there?"

"Whoever this hooded man is. It's got to be him. He's got us at each other's throats. You can't possibly believe I did it."

"The knife is in your room, Samantha."

"Why in the hell would I keep the knife in my room if I did it? That doesn't make any sense. I didn't kill dad. You have to believe me."

"I don't know what to believe anymore."

With that, Helen turned and walked away. Wesley watched her as she went. She seemed hollow. He had never seen her that way before. Looking down at Samantha, he spat and walked away, locking himself in his room.

Samantha struggled with her father's death. There was too much to process. In less than twenty-four hours, she had lost three family members and now the rest of her family thought she was a killer. She had nothing left. Samantha wanted nothing more than to end her misery right then and there but she couldn't, she wouldn't. Suicide would never be an option for her.

But she had to prove to her mother she hadn't killed her father. She couldn't lose her mother. After her dad had killed Tyler, she had been all right losing him from her life. But her mom, she was different. Her mother had always taken great care of her and loved her unconditionally. They had a special bond that a lot of mothers shared with their daughters. If she lost her mother from her life then it would truly be over. There would be nothing left for her in life. Then, she would have no idea how she would react.

Cracking the door open, she peered into the hallway. The coast was clear and she crept towards her mother's room. The house was eerily silent and she couldn't shake the feeling something terrible had happened. With her mouth dry and heart pounding, Samantha lightly rapped on her mother's door. When there was no answer she said, "Mom, can I come in. I need to talk to you. I didn't do it. I swear on my life I didn't do it. I need you to believe me. I can't lose you too."

Trying the doorknob, she realized it was open. What she found inside the bedroom shocked her to her very core. Dropping to her knees, she let out a terrified scream. Wesley came running to see what was wrong and stopped dead in his tracks. Hanging from the ceiling fan by a thin rope was the body of their mother.

"Jesus Fuck, no!" He cried and turned away. "This can't be happening."

Samantha sobbed on the floor until her throat was raw. That was it. Everything had been taken away from her in less than a day. Her whole family, apart from Wesley, was gone. Pressing her head against the cold floor, she cried.

XVII Towards Town

The next several hours were somber. Wesley and Samantha worked together to bury their entire family, including Tyler, in the clearing. Samantha had followed Wesley into the woods to retrieve Ashley's body. After seeing the gruesome scene, she had vomited for the second time that day.

Now, standing over three mounds of dirt in the clearing, the two survivors stood in silence. "We've got to get out of here and head into town," Samantha stated.

"Yeah, I should go anywhere with a killer," Wesley said as he started to walk away.

Samantha grabbed him by the wrist and said, "Wait, I know you don't believe me but I really didn't do it. But it doesn't matter. We need to leave this place and you can't do it alone."

"Watch me."

"No, you really can't. I have the map back to town and you have no idea how to read one."

He knew what she said was the truth but he thought on it for some time. "Maybe I can do my best to figure it out."

"Do you really want to risk it?"

He thought for several more minutes before responding, "Fine. You're right. I guess I need you, for now. But the moment we get back to civilization, you and I go our separate ways. I never want to see you again. Do you understand me? You're never going to see me again."

Tears welled up in her eyes and she nodded.

"Good. Let's get our shit together and get this over with."

Each of them packed a backpack and dropped them by the door. Making sure no essential items had been missed, the two of them headed out into the afternoon. Birds chirped happily all around them and the day was beautiful, but it was lost on them both.

The hike was quiet and awkward at first. For the moment, they were content pretending everything was alright. Everything would change in a couple of days, but it didn't matter.

The day carried on and they walked down the dirt road in silence. Samantha estimated the journey would take about three days. If they could walk non-stop, they might get done in two, but sleep and rest would take up a large portion of that time. It would be exhausting and neither liked the idea of sleeping in the open. If Tyler really had not been the killer, it meant the hooded man was still out there somewhere. He could be watching them at this very moment. But there was no other choice. They had to carry on.

The afternoon dragged on and the sun eventually slipped below the horizon. After a few more hours of hiking, they decided to pull off the road and set up a small camp. It wouldn't be anything fancy. A couple blankets and a small fire to keep animals away.

Samantha pulled out the lighter from her pack and got the fire going. Wesley spread out his blanket and Samantha did the same. They sat by the fire, not speaking a word. After about an hour, Wesley stretched his arms to the sky. "I think I'm going to try and sleep. The earlier we wake up, the quicker we get out of this terrible place."

She nodded in agreement. "You go ahead. I'm going to keep watch for a while. I don't feel comfortable out in the open like this." Wesley shrugged and laid back with his hands behind his head. As he did, his sleeve came up. At first, Samantha paid no attention. Instead, she stared at the fire and occasionally looked around.

When she did finally look over at her brother, she noticed something peculiar. Among the random bruises and scratches on his arm, there was one horizontal cut just below his shoulder. It looked deeper than the others, or so she thought. It could have been the light from the fire playing tricks on her, she wasn't sure. She stared at it for a long time and could only wonder at its existence.

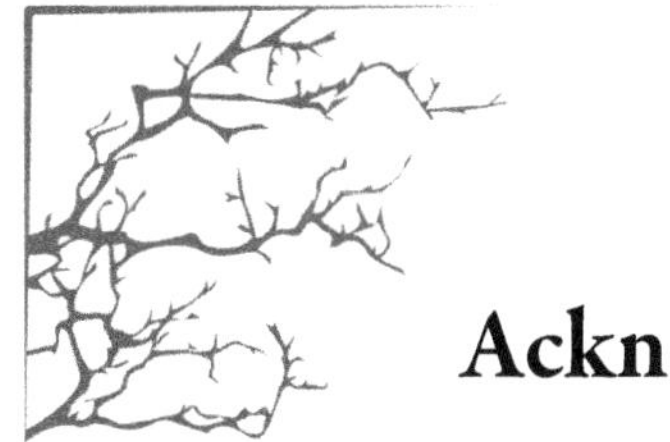

Acknowledgments

First of all, I have to thank you for choosing to read this book. Without you, I wouldn't have an audience in which to entertain. It means the world to me that you picked up my book and read it all the way through. Please consider leaving me a review on your preferred e-reader platform. It makes us authors feel good about ourselves and encourages others to read our work. So, thank you for your future review!

I also have to thank my wonderful patrons for their support. They make it possible for me to advertise my books and help pay for the book covers like this one. Thank you to Roxie Prince, Teresa Chaffee, and, my mother, Shari Bond. Your support means more than you can imagine.

As always, thanks to my graphic artist, Timothy Schmit, for another amazing book cover design, as well as reliable person to bounce my ideas off of. It helps keep my creative brain working. And I could never make the kind of art he does out of my book covers.

My wife's family deserves thanks as well for the camping trip which inspired this story. Of course, it wasn't my style of camping, but it was fun none-the-less. And it helped spark the idea of a murderous psychopath killing an entire family during a family getaway. But I swear, I like you guys!

Don't miss out!

Visit the website below and you can sign up to receive emails whenever Evan Bond publishes a new book. There's no charge and no obligation.

https://books2read.com/r/B-A-ZJVF-YDAS

Connecting independent readers to independent writers.

Did you love *Getaway*? Then you should read *Death Can Wait*[1] by Evan Bond!

[2]

A vacation to Brazil is everything Renee Walker thought it would be. Her and her husband, Luke, have an amazing time. Things get better when their friends invite them on their yacht for the return trip to the states. Luke and Renee relax as they make the slow, but wonderful journey home. They are all unprepared when a storm rips apart the yacht. During the mayhem, Luke and Renee are thrust overboard. Miraculously unharmed, they wash up on a deserted island. They work together to survive, scavenging for food and building shelter. Before too long, they realize the island is far from deserted. The inhabitants are bloodthirsty men who will stop at nothing to protect their island and take a

1. https://books2read.com/u/mVZGg5
2. https://books2read.com/u/mVZGg5

particular interest in Renee. For the first time in their lives, Luke and Renee are forced to survive.

Read more at https://www.evanbondauthor.com/.

About the Author

Evan Bond is a thriller/suspense author who loves blending his love of the outdoors with his writings. He is the author of the best selling psychological thriller *Echoes of the Past* and his intense action-packed survival account *Death Can Wait.* He has always had a passion for telling suspenseful stories. Even at a young age, he was crafting horror stories to share with his family and friends. Evan Bond lives in Tampa, Florida with his wife, Melissa, their two boys, Desmond and Logan, and their cat and dog, Whiskey and Loki. When he's not writing, he can be found adventuring in the outdoors with his family and calling it "research" for his next novel.

Read more at https://www.evanbondauthor.com/.

www.ingramcontent.com/pod-product-compliance
Ingram Content Group UK Ltd.
Pitfield, Milton Keynes, MK11 3LW, UK
UKHW022006190726
13853UKWH00004B/1769

9 798330 383139